Ribstone Pippins

Helen Wykham

Marion Boyars
London · New York

This paperback edition first published
in Great Britain and the United States
in 1997 by Marion Boyars Publishers
24 Lacy Road, London SW15 1NL
237 East 39th Street, New York NY 10016

Distributed in Australia and New Zealand by
Peribo Pty Ltd, 58 Beaumont Road, Mount Kuring-gai, NSW.

First published in hardcover by Allen Figgis & Co.Ltd., Dublin,
in conjunction with Calder & Boyars, London, 1974.
© Allen Figgis & Co. Ltd 1974, 1997

British Library Cataloguing in Publication Data
Wykham, Helen
   Ribstone pippins : a novel
   1. Teenage girls — Sexual behaviour —
   Fiction 2. Humorous stories
   I. Title
   823.9'14[F]

Library of Congress Cataloging-in-Publication Data
   Wykham, Helen.
      Ribstone Pippins : a novel / by Helen Wykham.
      p. cm.
      I. Title
   PR6073.Y5R53   1997
   823'.914--dc21
                                           97–29418
                                              CIP

ISBN 0–7145–3017–4 Paperback

Printed by Athenaeum Press, Gateshead, England

to J. G., in lieu

I said to Heart, 'How goes it?' Heart replied:
'Right as a Ribstone Pippin!' But it lied.

Hilaire Belloc

Letter xliv

Dear Aileen,

Coming to work today I passed this apple tree in this private garden, and it reminded me of Belloc's little rhyme. It has been running around in my head all morning, and I feel as if I will never shake it out. It occurs to me that for the last three years I have heaped indignities upon you and the apple trees have propelled me into an almost neurotic state of confessionalism, if there is such a word! (Sp?) So I am going to write you out the tale of the Ribstone Pippins, which is a sorry tale, a pale little tale, but nonetheless there, and all the tale there is. The misery of writing it all out on the Municipal headed paper will be my sparse gesture to you for these last years. It merits no acceptance, needing none. Pray handle it with discretion.

Yours,
Helen

MOTHER

I SAT with my sister beyond the rails of overcoats in the coffee room of Brown Thomas' in Dublin. I was terrified of Stephanie in those days, and, frankly, I still am. She is called Stephanie because Mother, in her usual lavish way, confused the grand issues of life and death, and believing herself to be dying when in fact she was giving birth, directed that the child should be named after her second husband, Stephen Wykham, our father (perhaps as a reminder of something). Predictably, Mother did not die then; she died last year in Perugia, massively wealthy, and our last step-father sent me her last wedding ring on a gilt chain. Stephanie and Mother were very alike; they both had lush brown, bobbed hair, and the sort of limbs that look magnificent in white belted raincoats with elaborate shoulder flaps. Many of Mother's rejected suitors had a go at Stephanie, which was no doubt how she acquired her somewhat liberal education.

Myself, I was doing sums on the pink damask table-cloth. For the third time running I made it sixty weeks and four days since I had last seen Lyn. Sixty weeks and four days since the start of the school half-term from which she never came back. There had been rumours, about a man, of course, but I obliterated them. I only knew that she was still alive, and I unable to experience it. Last week, crossing London at the end of term, for like all my kind I was educated in England, I had been in Paddington station. The loudspeaker had been blaring, and suddenly screamed at me, at me personally, ' . . . the next train from Platform 3, calling at Salisbury . . . '; she lived in Upavon. I had been there. From Salisbury you take the Marlborough bus north along the Avon valley, through Amesbury and Durrington, and get off where you see the water-meadows below and the village same schools as each other and their language sent a frisson up my spine. We never entertained them on Fridays because of the fish, and not very often on other days, but they frequently had us, well watered down in numbers, to their bigger parties.

Stephanie said anxiously, 'But you like Anna, don't you? She rides.'

'She does. And I do like her. But she's not much fun. She always looks as if she were up for auction, with no buyers.' I was told off for that, which meant that I had hit the nail on the head and also that I wasn't going to get out of it, although the very idea of me at a house-party was patently ridiculous. It didn't sound like my Thing at all. It would be frightening, and full of frightening people talking French. Most people were frightening to me then.

'I take it you'll be there?' I asked nervously.

'Good lord, yes. Wouldn't miss it for anything!' No, I supposed not.

I supposed, too, that obviously they wouldn't let me go alone. I'd never get the titles right, let alone the cutlery. I had a momentary flash of excitement when the titles came into my head—they were very long, French and harsh and I would like to have been a footman so that I could call them out at a reception, or a man so that I could use them in introductions. 'It's a complicated affair,' Stephanie explained. I had already guessed that it must be if they needed me in on it. 'Maria has this cousin, from France or England or somewhere, who's a. the head of the family and frightfully grand (at least, I suppose he must be); b.' (she was ticking the items off on her fingers, to be sure she didn't underestimate the Augustitude of the Cousin) 'b. he's stinking rich and

Maria's bankrupt again and has to sell her Sèvres—'
(her what?) 'and c. he's a bachelor and young. So you
see.'

I saw. 'But why me?' I persisted, doggedly.

'Because you're Anna's age, of course, and my sister,
and know French, and you're supposed to be clever,
and she knows you.'

Also I was unattractive, nobody much in that set-up,
but very respectable in name, and a Protestant; so I
wasn't likely to be a threat to anyone. But Stephanie?
'How many people?'

'I don't know. Topsy Geary is one, and I rather think
Peter, unfortunately.'

They must have been unengaged for over three months
now, so I thought that that might be all right. 'Why
Peter?'

'Maria thinks she may be going to have to sell her
Lalique collections, too, and Peter's mother has an old
uncle who's just died.'

I saw that as well. Dublin works like that. 'O God,' I
thought, resignedly, 'Thou knowest how busy we shall
be that week . . .' It still didn't sound like much of a
party. Or not my idea of a party.

'I think I'm too immature,' I said hopefully. 'It's
obviously going to be riddled with fraught emotions,
Jane Austen plots and underground sexual currents which
I am quite incapable of dealing with.' (I thought that was
rather good, I must remember it for Topsy, if the worst
came to the worst.)

Stephanie giggled. 'You can be quite funny,' she said
kindly. 'I'm hoping that it'll be all of those things, it
would be hilarious. Now if you talk like that instead of
about horses, cut your hair and leave your trousers

behind, you may get a lot of fun out of it. You may even BE fun. And you're quite nice looking, you're very like Daddy.'

I couldn't see how that made me nice looking, but I let it pass. I was more worried about her expectations that I might be fun. I was never "fun." I'm still not "fun." One strange face and my tongue swelled, my hands grew to gargantuan proportions, my bosom and bottom became objects of national ridicule, and my only source of conversation lay in the safe haven of equine exploits, unambiguous, and definitely not fraught. Not fraught at all.

'We're going to buy you some clothes,' my unrealistic sister went on, 'here, as soon as Mother comes.'

'You can't,' I said flatly.

'Why not?'

'My bra is dirty, and my—'

'O, my God, look at that, will you!' The inelegance of Stephanie's drooping jaw provoked me to whip round on my little satin chair.

He was walking in behind our mother. The brilliant neon caught up the reddy colour of his hair and turned it to viscous flame; flared in the depths of his eyes, burning like holy oil. He hesitated for a thousand years, glancing around the room, looking for someone—the closed, complicated face of him below the fires like an angel of Jaweh. An iron angel among the overcoats. The earth trembled when he walked past our table, to pass out of sight behind me. Rising from out of the great silence of his passing, I heard the thunderous clamour of the middle classes taking morning coffee. Like any other pole-axed animal, I bowed my mute head and traced clover leaves in the pink damask.

'. . . pheasant feathers, darling, not bantam,' Mother

was saying. Most deeply shocked to find her secular presence here in this Burning Ground, I looked up at her with blinded eyes—and winced. I realised what Stephanie had been referring to.

'You mark my words, blue and green will be in next month.' I marked them, burned with a branding iron into the scorched flesh of my left arm where his hip had brushed me. In the exotic, super-sensual perception of those moments I understood for the first time that I adored my mother. I cannot even now smell Cona coffee and rich pastry without thinking of Mother in her plumage. She was an outrage, and I adored her for it. All my later memories of subsequent step-fathers, hotel meetings that began with Cinzano and the latest batch of step-siblings and ended with those fabulous green Lloyd's cheques, of Italian brilliances and potted palms and hasty air-terminal meetings, cannot compare in clarity with that appalling moment in BT's when, with an Iron Angel like the wall of God behind my back, I sat with my sister and, for the first time, I admired my mother. She was an outrage. And her hat feathers were real pheasant.

'Helen, dear, do you feel all right? Because if you don't we must go. Indeed, if you do we must in any case go. I must buy you shoes and panties.'

So we paid where the Holy Fires had played, and I did not look back, as we went out past the rails of overcoats, did not look over my shoulder as we marched in echelon to the Lingerie.

'—No, no, something much—much frothier; she'd just look silly if she were run over and stranded in an ambulance in eau-de-nil. Look again—'

Nor did I look back as we went down the stairs and

17

through the glittering costume jewellery and portentious gold-topped bottles, with Mother, my magnificent mother, striding in front like a peacock in her blue and green of next month, out into the hot street below the tall Georgian windows. She glittered most fearsomely amongst the silks. And I carried my fragile new knickers in pink tissue amongst the drunken splendour of the first morning of Horse Show Week.

'—No, no, something a fraction heavier; those calves look silly above an ankle strap that size—'

No, no: no, no. Look again. She will look silly in eau-de-nil on the ambulance stretcher; she will look silly on the dry, hard pavements in a tiny worked shoe designed for the likes of her elegant sister; she will look silly anyway, for she on honey-dew might feed.

▣

'Stephanie; Stephanie, please!'

She was perched on a shelf, doing something totally mysterious and unspeakably feminine to, of all places, her knees. Her dress was draped about her thighs, and I could see the dark triangular shadow in her pants. Averting my eyes in horror, I heaved at my breasts.

'O, God, O Stephanie.'

She looked up in astonishment at my contortions, my huddled posture, my grotesque pain. Irritated she said, 'Oh, stand up Helen. You look so silly like that.' Spitting with rage and despair I straightened to see me me me me me all down the long room in all the long mirrors, strip-lit on the backs of the penny-in-slot doors. God; who'd ever think of bringing pennies to a Hunt Ball? God, I want to pee—

'Stephanie!'

'O—'

'I haven't any pennies, and I want to pee. Often. Lots of pees—'

'For crying out loud! Will you behave. There are people in some of those. Here, you can have two of mine.'

Two? Only two pees all night? Somebody should have told me . . .

'What's the matter with you anyway?'

'Everything,' I grovelled.

'You need a drink.' (No, no; only two pennies, or only a short one anyway. Short and very strong. Schnapps, or vodka or ipecacuanha, whatever they might be. They all sounded very short and very strong. I yearned). To give her her due, Stephanie abandoned her knees to my enormous relief and started on my eyebrows. To my dismay. Obediently I stood while the hard pencil drew an expression suitable to that of a Young Girl at her First Public Ball, upon my beetling brow. I had Come Out that year, an operation attended to with tremendous precision by Mother, aqueous in periodot and pearls, with a cleft in her bosom from which she arose like a Venus who had never heard of Botticelli. Mother's launching of her backward fledgling had been a social *prix d'estime*. Even Stephanie had not had a look-in beside Mother on the night of my Coming Out. Wondering exactly how to Go back In again without jeopardising Mother's career, I was consequently immobile when one of Stephanie's beastlier pals swept up to us trilling endearments and floating upon an enviable flushing sound that made my corset retract with a twitch.

I said 'Hi!'

Stephanie hissed savagely, 'You can't say that here.'

I had read it in a book. If not here, then where? I would say it as often as possible.

The friend closed in on me, crying, 'Helen, I didn't recognise you! Stephanie did you choose her dress?' She stooped to examine my out-stretched hand. 'Goodness, is that your old engagement ring? O Stephanie, honestly, you are—!' My knees dripped about my insoles in icy dissolution.

'Is it? Is it Peter's ring?' I beseeched, tugging frantically at it.

She inherited that chuckle in straight descent from Machiavelli. 'Put it back, he won't be here.'

O God. Now and in the hour of our death.

I followed them out of that satin coffin into the foyer. The first thing I observed was that it stank. It stank of champagne and feet and whiskey and flowers, and because I am short I could only see an impenetrable mesh of nudity and soft black cloth (I am of that height which puts my eyes on a level with the average tie knot). No possible place of egress. Miraculously, or because she was tall, Stephanie steered us to our party without hesitation, and I managed to focus for long enough to register dismay. It was a carefully constructed affair. Quite obviously Mother had had my innocence in mind when she organised the party. It was significantly lacking in Exciting People, Roman Catholic People and Questionable People.

So I discussed current Dublin Theatre with a funny little chap I knew as Owen Blank, who indiscriminately chatted up my mother and my sister at cocktail parties, warmly pressed to his budding *embonpoint* and his palpable memories of Stephanie. I quickstepped with athletic leaps among the happy, hunched couples who had Dined together and were therefore on intimate terms before Supper; I foxtrotted to gay tales of the tennis-club party with one who had scared the pants off me since I was eleven, before it was realised that I couldn't even see the ball, much less be induced to hit it; and was left with Henry. Henry was my second cousin twice removed on the distaff side, and he was doing a course in Dairying. He was about as much of a social lightning flash as I was. We waltzed. We tangoed. We Gay Gordoned. We waltzed again. I disregarded Mother's instructions and produced a packet of cigarettes. He didn't smoke. I talked about cows, but he had had enough of shop. I talked about cars. He didn't drive. I talked about courtesans, and he went to the gents. I contemplated Popping Out of my Bra, an activity guaranteed to throw even the Gardai, much less Henry, but I didn't know how to pop in again. Hunt Balls, balls, I thought.

So I watched the meetings and matchings that would result in a liaison or two, a sorrow or two, a marriage or two, and no suicides. It didn't seem to have anything very much to do with me or Lyn. I wouldn't marry as a result of this Horse Show Week. Or the next. Or the next. I wondered if one got drunk before supper, or whether such a search for oblivion was a strictly post-prandial activity in the etiquette book. I worried about it slightly before deciding to take immediate action. The result was good. I decided to do it again. Tomorrow night, for example. Or sooner—

'Enjoying yourself?'

'Gracious, yes, Tony. Of COURSE I am!'

'Then come and do the Charleston with me.'

Ha! Ha—ha! Hi. This was something I could do. Something I was good at. We did it a lot at the end of that interminable decade. It was my one sporting accomplishment, and the way I did it, it required no team spirit. That night I was very good indeed. Pom-pom. Pom-pom. Pom ta ta tiddy pa—ta (?) Open space around—Wooops ta-ta tiddy, (?) too much; Tony?

O GOD.

Inside a jigging, watching circle. They gave us plenty of room. Me and Him. My Iron Angel from among the overcoats in Brown Thomas'. Quick, faster than me; prrump pam-pam ti-pa; economical, neat, team-spirited, watching with tremendous concentration every move I made, matching, complementing, supplementing; his lips moving slightly—Pom-pom. Pom-pom. Ta ra ra tada Da. Maybe a Dervish could tell you how I did for the rest of that dance. I can't remember. The end. The bitter silence of the end. Some spasmodic laughter, and a clap or two. They often clap the Jesters. A drop of sweat trickled down beside his mouth. I felt it also beside mine and licked it away.

'Thank you very much,' he said. I smiled at the closed face. I observed that his braces were embroidered. I observed that his eyes were dead and that his trouser band was too loose. I saw that he was cut off somewhere just behind the flesh and that his fingers were too long.

'It was a pleasure,' I said. It was my first adult moment when I turned away from him into a world suddenly a nonsense of lilies and lifelessness, to find Tony. And not to find Lyn.

◩

I went to the Horse Show obsessively every day. Not, as hitherto, to fall in love with a Ladies Hack, as I had done annually since I was eight, but to find an Iron Angel among the thousands. God knows how I expected to find him among the thousands. I put on the clothes Stephanie and Mother had chosen for me, though somewhat resenting the hat, took my parasol in my hand and went on my quest. My parasol was a wonderful thing; it was my only affectation. It was white with green roses; it was utterly frivolous; it was pretty and altogether utterly frivolous. It was getting grimy, and I remember wondering, how on earth do you wash a parasol.

Each day I walked in beauty through the Great Main Entrance which proclaimed the Royal Dublin Society. The Royal Dublin Society for the brightest dahlia in the Free State; the fattest turkey in the Free State; for Children's Art and the Amadeus Quartet; for the equine, literary, agricultural and social *élite* in the Free State. I ransacked the Stallions' Boxes, the Flower Show, the Jumping Horses Only, the queues outside the gents, the queues outside the bars, the Harness Classes and the bandstands. He was not in any of those places when I was. I pressed through foaming flanks and This Year's Colour, trod on dropped buttonholes and glowing carnations among the dung and the cobbles. About me the meetings became assignations; the matchings, matings. Diamonds changed hands under the stunted planes. Almost everything that was going had gone, because now it was Thursday lunchtime and only one day was left. And I was left, standing alone under the Clock (tick-tock, don't wake me up), and so was Maria SanFé, Lady Calary.

Under the Clock is where you stand when you are being stood up and are pretending that you have confused times. I had good reason to know. I'd spen t a large part of many successive Horse Shows there.

Above the hush of expectant soliloquies, Lady Calary's harsh tenor rang out like a belch in Church. 'What the hell do you mean, playing the organ? What organ? Whose organ?'

Maria SanFé was well known not so much as a pillar of society but as one of its more grotesque embellishments. I was beginning to be old enough to see why. Right now she was beginning to make the pillars lean. Her companion evidently made some mollifying answer, for she said, disconcertingly, 'O, Handel's organ. That's different. I should have enjoyed hearing that. He should have told me.'

The imagination balked at the picture of Maria SanFé rearing about on her flat heels in the grey funereal Church that houses Dublin's greatest musical souvenir. Suitably impressed by the proximity of a Great Gift, I eavesdropped shamelessly with the rest. After all, one could wait a little if it was Handel's organ that was being manipulated—

Profundo into the lull, 'Great God of Israel. I'm lunching. Now.' And away with her, chestnut eyebrows swarming inside her veil (a hunting one, I noticed, attached superfluously to a felt cloche, worn as a bowler, and just short enough to permit a cigarette to be lit with minimum risk of a blaze). I observed that her objective was not the Members' Luncheon Rooms but the Members' Bar and thought that the organist would not have to be very perspicacious to find her.

I had already decided that even the titles and the sensation of conversing by the thousand acre was not going to be worth it. I had told Mother so at breakfast. I had said with unwonted severity, through a bird's nest which seemed to have been constructed overnight in the roof of my mouth, that I considered Stephanie's

24

(and Mother's, but I didn't say that out loud) way of looking at marriage—decide what you want and no holds barred till you got a man to give it to you inside the law and the conventions—to be fine. I was all for it. But to impose the attitude on someone else, to try and marry your daughter to some stinking rich posh cousin so that you could buy back your Sèvres, whatever they might be, next time the banks gave you a cheque-book was immoral. Much moved by my rectitude I had refused fried eggs for the first time on record (it was also my first hang-over). Stephanie had my eggs as well as her own and looked wicked. Mother had leaned her long back against the Aga, tucked her emery file behind her ear, and weighed in with a lengthy, masculine lecture on the facts of financial life, dowries, land tenure, inbreeding, primogeniture, Gilt-Edged, and birth-control-as-practised-by-the-R.Cs. and ended up with a flourish by whacking the copper omelette pan from Prisunic's that hung on the wall, saying, 'And anyway, the SanFés are French.'

I couldn't see any connection but nodded wisely to stop her launching forth on Salic Law or settlement which logically came next. I was aware that in some way my objections had been overruled.

I cocked a snook in the direction of the plunging bowler *manqué* and set off for the Exhibition Hall. I had something to do, and I had borrowed Stephanie's biggest hat to do it in. I had imbibed with my bottle the knowledge that honesty is not an economic policy. Mother had brought us up to be very economical, no doubt because of her awareness that security is not a blessing renowned for longevity. Not that Mother was dishonest (she was, but on such a lavish scale that it became a different category of vice altogether), but Stephanie and I were.

25

At the end of the Hall, down a thousand yards of coconut matting, size, Irish Ropes, Waterford Glass, hessian, draught, tweed and one's relatives ('You did WHAT with your dahlia?—Oh, a prize, I must have misheard you!'), the big newspapers have their stalls, and the photographs taken at the Hunt Balls at night, and in the Show Ground by day, are pinned up for all the world and his wife to enjoy. Most of them referred to Money and Quality, and they were for sale. I had a quick check. Amongst all the forgotten smiles, fractional incidents, discarded encounters, and episodes lost in a multiplicity of episodes, my Iron Angel's mask was not hard to find. There were seven altogether. Only one was within brim-reach. Since I had reached financial exhaustion I had regretfully to let the other six go. One can, of course, buy the prints. Acquisition otherwise, however, is not difficult. It's a question of so arranging the hat-brim that sooner or later one gets jostled against the board by the hundreds who have come to see if they are represented. Two or three photographs come down together. One grovels among the feet and brolly stems on the floor, because one can't get anything for nothing, and emerges, undignified but oh so honest, with the important print in one's catalogue, well hidden, and hands the others back. I did it every year for my Ladies' Hack.

Smiling bashfully I faded out to the least claustrophobic of the public Ladies and, having paid a penny for my privacy, spread the *Irish Times* on the seat and sat upon it. Immediately the sweat started around the hair line. My hands turned to gross bunches of *wurst*, tied at one end. My thighs spreadeagled among the suspenders. I dropped the catalogue, programme, parasol and new gloves on the puddled tile floor. The stall stank of other people's pee.

The back of the catalogue was corrugated with anonymous wet. I had one cigarette for emergencies, so I lit it. After half of it my fingers were reduced to mere frankfurter size. The attendant slapped and whisked about the basins. Someone rattled the door. "Eileen Loves Kevin" juddered to the irritation of Her Outside. I balanced the remainder of the cigarette on the toilet roll and turned over the photograph. I don't know how long I sat there, admiring the beautiful face on the illustration. A church brass of a man long dead. There is a joke here somewhere, but I can't see it.

◙

I don't know how long I sat there, wondering at the beautiful face in the illustration. A church brass of a man long dead . . . the dead are so graceful, being wonderless . . .

' . . . not havin' me Ladies Cloaks used as a smokin' cave be bold young girdles . . .'

I said 'Fuck off' for the first time in my life, and crept out into the sunlight under the clock. Tick-tock, don't wake me up——

◙

That afternoon, wherever I looked, he was there.

And again that night amongst the thousands at the Ball . . .

◙

And again on the final day, among the pipe bands, and the thousands . . . Tick-tock, tick tock, I cannot stop the ticking clock

He came late to the Ball that final night, with an opera programme in his pocket, tawny in the bracken colours of some stag pack, the only golden one in all the pinks and blacks. The revolving lights blazed on the great crested buttons, and I stood with Topsy Geary on a balcony while her partner threw bread rolls at his best friend. I held her hand and watched my mother. And my mother watched my Iron Angel, for she was in the same party, no doubt at the invitation of Marc-Raoul, who it seemed was about to become my next and second step-father. Anna SanFé and Maria SanFé were in the party too. They came with the French Ambassador and did not throw bread rolls. And my mother's eyes and my eyes met on the only golden one in all that brilliant throng, flaming wherever we looked. At dawn they sounded the hunting horns, and the last strident cacophony of the winter call was bloodier and baser than ever brass had sounded out before.

◻

That night my mother did not come home. Nor did my sister.

◻

Traffic jams all down O'Connell Street
the visitors are leaving
Stand-by tickets for the London, Glasgow, Bristol planes, for the Irish Mail
the visitors are leaving
the visitors have left
I am left. Alone. I am tired. I turn home to Lyn.

DOMINIC

'SHERRY, MISS. Medium or dry?'

'Oh. Oh—dry. Yes. Thank-you,' I said hastily, into my cigarette. I hadn't worked out the technique of talking while it was in your mouth, and Peter was watching closely to see if 1 had worked out the technique. 'Definitely dry,' I added.

Fascinated, I watched the pale gilt swim up the glass. I watched Peter's glass fill with a more robust looking hue and knew I had made a mistake. I dithered for lack of Stephanie. She was a hundred miles away, looking like a throw-back to our silk-importing merchant forebears. Her gleaming eyes were gone a-roving up and down the pale cold room, up and down the dark distant portraits, up and down the faded embroidered curtains, up and down the hard polished floor, the fecundity of the plaster flora in the high cornices. A-roving, too, up and down the guests. Like a ship swinging to anchor, Peter gyrated about me in his efforts to keep her in sight as she prowled from one to another of the tall men and the tall women. It was appalling. We were brought up on carpets, in Dalkey. Also, we swept the cob-webs out of the corners (tho' they were not so high, it is true).

'How was the Show then, Helen?' I wished Peter wouldn't adopt that jocular tone. It was the sort of tone you have to adopt when talking to your was-to-have-been young sister-in-law.

'Topping,' 1 said, unimaginatively. Six nights ago I had been wearing their engagement ring. He deserved better than this. 'I love it, you know. One sees horse flesh as it really can be. And the jumping—every one of them with those low, springy hocks!'

'Really. Did you go to the balls?'

'Good heavens, yes. Great gas, the balls. Balls.' I added reflectively, 'I came out this year.'

'I know.'

Defeated we both watched Stephanie making a tour from the double doors at the hall end of the gargantuan enclosure referred to by the servants as the Drawing Room, past Topsy, whom she ignored, past Lady Calary who was slouched with her shoulders rubbing dreamily against the Adam fireplace, her eyes unfocussed in the general direction of her drink which was significantly different-looking from ours. Her top lip was raised in a sort of sick amiability, and she shifted on heavy feet as Stephanie progressed past her. I was more interested in her companion. She looked about forty-five and had the pale, high face of a ballerina. Some structural quality held my attention, as with a painting to which one will presently come at the far end of a gallery. Peter minced about my left arm; Stephanie had inspected and dismissed the overgrown boy behind the sofa-table. He looked as if he were trying to hide, and I felt a spasm of sympathy for his clumsy movements. He could not have been much older than I, I thought, and he seemed not to have slept for some time. Covertly I sidled out behind Peter, just as Stephanie, ringless and dispassionate, arrived with her usual air of spurious intimacy. I left them to it, wishing them good luck with the low-slung hocks, or whatever ex-es talk about after Horse Show Week in Dublin. I took a great gulp of the sherry. O GOD. It would have to be medium next time; my top lip stretched with the bitter drought of it. I headed for the fireplace where Anna, tiny and tightly drawn, was quietly arranging cheese straws on a mutilated dish.

'Hello,' she said. 'Are you all right? Have a straw.'

She held them delicately to my hand, and obediently I took one. 'I don't suppose Ma has introduced you to anyone. She never does.' Carefully she altered her arrangement to take account of the void left by the cheese straw I was munching. 'Nor do I.'

'Most of them look as if they are your cousins,' I remarked, taking another.

Anna sighed, and started again, on a triangular theme this time. 'Most of them are.'

I decided that the feeling in my belly was definitely nasty and wondered if a diet of cheese straws and dry sherry would cure it. I thought it might. Anna resignedly allowed me one and then slipped quietly away to less philistine palates. I clutched the tiny thing and glared around, defensive and alone. Topsy had beaten me to Gollylocks behind the table and was doing her About-To-Become-An-Art-Student act with a moderate degree of success. She had left school. She was O.K. was our Topsy. She had a great motto. It went, 'Nothing Succeeds Like Success'. I had no motto and veered off round the chimney-breast (quite a walk) where I came to roost in great unease. This feeling was exaggerated by a very ancient, high-backed chair standing uncompromisingly square to the wall. You didn't tilt back in that one and rest your boots on the miniature fluted columns. Behind me the babble thawed a little, and even Maria's rasping tenor could be heard swilling about below the chattering. O, God.

'Interested?'

I jumped as if I'd been caught trying to get out of Remedials.

'No, no,' I cried. 'I mean, yes. O, God.'

'My name,' he said, 'is Matthew. Matthew Frost.'

'How nice.' How nice of him to tell me. How nice of him to put his enormous bulk between me and the party. How nice of him to have such dark, lacustrine eyes on each side of his huge, broken nose. How nice of him to be six foot six, ugly, and talking to me. 'How nice.'

'Yes,' he said, 'it's Jacobean.'

'What is?'

'The chair.'

I said 'Oh' and 'I'm Helen Wykham. Stephanie's sister.'

His great eyes encompassed me, drawing me up to at least the Standard Average Size for British Females.

'And who might she be?' he asked anxiously.

'Dry, wasn't it, miss?'

I shrivelled back to Thumbelina height. His name was Grogan, or Mr. Grogan. I wasn't sure which. And he was a butler. We didn't have a butler. This gave him the right to dictate my taste in sherry. He knew it; I knew that he knew, etc.

'Medium,' I contradicted, rudely.

'Oh yes, miss? I had thought it was dry.'

Dark and robust the medium glowed forgivingly in the decanter, fractionally withheld from me in my uncertainty. 'Oh, medium, it was medium!' I cried, hitching my fingers over the tell-tale residue, so pale and unpalatable in the bottom of my glass. Mr. Grogan conceded. It was a Pyrrhic victory. Exhausted, I turned to Matthew Frost who had decently looked away and was examining a portrait on the wall. Of a man. That man. With long fingers to his ruff and a long complicated face . . .

'Gervase SanFé, 1557,' he was saying, peering at the writing beneath the frame. 'It's a nice piece, isn't it, Helen Wykham? But lifeless.'

In the void of silence which I had become, my

tummy rumbled. One of those that starts off with a high whine and descends to a gurgle. Shock, or sherry. Horrified, my eyes locked in Matthew Frost's.

'It may be that Dominic has forgotten that people do eat sometimes; or it may be that he has remembered and is flirting with Cook in the gun-room in the hopes of inducing her to issue us with edible rations, thereby defeating his own immediate ends, since the celery is burning and the meat unbasted. I wouldn't know. But in either eventuality, cheese straws would make an adequate addition to this excellent sherry. I shall now go and procure us some.'

'Do you play the organ?' I asked, inspired.

'No. I played the triangle once in the O.T.C. band at school. But in this company it is a trifling accomplishment.'

'The triangle?'

'Yes, the triangle. A silly little thing, really. It was too small for me.'

O God! The laughter burst like an explosion within me as he gravely removed his temendous bulk to search for cheese straws. So merry did I become that I sauntered over to Stephanie in an almost natural fashion. Long live the Spaniards, I cried to my ringing head, sing Hi! at every corner on the long and dusty road . . .

'Helen, this is Portland Fitzgarry. My sister Helen.' (and who might she be?).

I said Hi! and stuck out my hand. Stephanie recoiled visibly, but this Portland chap was all right, too. He was also very tall, like everyone else except Anna and me, but thin and droopy, and he had protruding wrist-bones and a bright red cummerbund to match them. He said, 'Hi! You'd better call me Bill. It's an irresistible temptation not worth fighting. My father is a geologist,

35

and my younger brother is called Chert, which is slightly worse.'

Enraptured, I gazed at him. Matthew Frost came back with a plateful of nameless sticky things, and I gazed at him too. Quite, quite bewitching. Another dose of definitely medium, and Stephanie might even be right. It was conceivable that I might even have fun. At which cue Lady Calary sounded out *fortissimo* for another round of drinks. Quite, quite enchanting, the way she was draped against the mantel, in her long black garment, angular, mysterious, she reminded me of the veiled altar furniture during Holy Week.

How enchanting to play excerpts from *Parsifal* in that black garment. What was it, a curtain?

'Do you play the organ?' I asked Portland Bill.

'Infrequently. And never on Sundays.'

We were rescued from this negative note by an English girl (it shows, in Dublin) with a hungry look. On closer inspection I noticed that she had little lines around her eyes, made by fear. I wondered who might have frightened her, for she had a peculiar beauty that was hard and bright, like strong filigree or wire in moonlight. She tucked her black hair behind her ear, gracelessly, and took half of Matthew's plate of stickinesses without a word. Challengingly, Matthew said, 'Harriet, I must beseech you to do something about your foster-brother. This person, Helen, is starving. I am positive that he is the cause of the delay. He has not yet been punctual for a single trivial or tremendous occasion. I begin to resent starving while he examines the local flora, rewires the dove cot, reads five chapters of Trevelyan, or however it may be that he employs the time between the sounding of the gong and his appearances.'

36

'It's not my fault. I'm famished, too. Half a hen leg for lunch and no breakfast. My tummy's been sounding out like a Thompson sub-machine gun since five o'clock. But what I resent, and quite bitterly at that, is not getting my tea. I like tea at four—'

'But if you come down to the woods, to the woods, with me tomorrow, you will find that I have purchased a little tin billy-can and a large jar of American coffee powder—'

Christ Jesus, the voice he had! O Christ, that voice . . .

'Laurie, where the hell have you been? They're all ganging up on me because you keep us from what little we hope to get—where have you been?'

'I've been in the cellar,' said my Iron Angel, stepping around me, and brushing whitewash off his shoulders on to mine. Mine were naked and burned with the quick-lime. 'I received a curious directive that we were about to consume "fowl from that water, there", which I interpreted as meaning that Maria had shot the last small moorhen with her bow and arrow, and would I look out a suitable accompaniment in the wine cellar. Not having heard of most of the outrageous things down there, I had to take a reference book, to look up what might be Full Bodied to augment the fowl. I'm sorry if I'm late, I would hate to appear inhospitable.'

'What you mean,' Matthew Frost grumbled at him, 'is that you found a nice private place to read in and have been sitting on an upturned beer-barrel, studying *Beano*.'

'Not *Beano*. I do assure you it wasn't *Beano*. But forgive me . . . ' his eyebrow flickered again and we all watched him as he went to Maria, crucified against the empty hearth, her long, bare arms outstretched along

37

the mantelpiece. She condensed as he approached, assuming a crouching pose, waiting. He did not appear to take her very seriously (how gracefully he walked, as it might have been a dancer, or a swordsman. Or Gervase 1557).

'Ah, Dominic,' she remarked. 'You've time for a glass—Grogan, give him some of that vinegar he drinks.' But Grogan was already there, for Grogan was a butler, and he had a special glass, on a special salver, with a different decanter on it. And it was accepted with the mild politeness I used towards Mother at supper time. My knees were wet with desire and greed.

Maria glared at us. We came, even Harriet, to sub-standard attention. 'Now, who d'you not know?'

He made a minimal gesture, amused, urbane.

'Well that one is Topsy Geary. I think she's an art student. Are you an art student, Topsy? And this is Peter Bartley-Drummond. The Glass Industry. He used to be engaged to that one there, and now he isn't. Most unsettling for hostesses. Those are the Wykham girls, Monica's daughters, you know.'

He nodded to indicate that he did indeed know (what?) and winked at Stephanie. I swelled up all over, definitely the time for more sherry. Can't consort with Angels sober.

Anna said quietly, 'O Ma, it's not a cattle show.' But Lady Calary refused to take correction. She formed up for the Crucifixion again but used him as part of the cross-bar this time. She made a funny little caressing gesture on his shoulder, nostalgic rather than affectionate. 'My cousin, Laurence SanFé, the Dominic,' she declared, like a loudspeaker van.

Unembarrassed, he looked at her. Then he smiled (O God, the smile he had) and murmured, 'Nor is it a stud parade, Maria.'

But she only said 'Ha!' and grinned like a proud stable lad. 'Give me a cigarette, Dominic, I've run out again.'

'So will I at this rate. Francis, there ought to be a new packet on the hall table, would you mind?'

So the golden haired boy left Topsy and a minute later was standing beside him, holding out the bright, new packet. While I watched, too astonished to comment, Harriet put it into words, suddenly giggling and muttering to Bill, 'Bill, look. They're like the Crazy Gang. They are all six exactly the same!'

And they were. Dominic SanFé, Anna SanFé, Francis (Sanfé? must be), the ballerina, Maria SanFé and Gervase 1557, under whom they clustered. And I loved her in the sherry for noticing Gervase, too. Fortunately we very soon went in to dinner.

And that was frightful, for the duck were certainly very small, and he made little exasperated gestures as he carved them with Grogan. The wine was certainly very Full Bodied, and he licked his lips like a satisfied gambler when Grogan gave him his little bit to taste, smiling slyly at Matthew and daring him to comment. And all the time he sat at the end of the miles of table in this vast black armchair, casually as if it had been carved for him, found satisfactory and fallen into familiar usage. And again I knew greed and desire among the other things, that he should sit like a quiet king at that end of the table which I knew was never used, for Maria like Mother was a widow. A stranger among us, come in from elsewhere, to a place left vacant against his coming. Through all that long dinner, I don't think I looked at him once. Through all that long dinner, I don't think I missed a word he spoke or a gesture he made.

Letter xlv

My life is so simple now that I find it hard to remember how it could have been with me that summer of Dominic. It is such a long time since I knew or cared who is President of the Jockey Club, so long since I tipped a housemaid or worried about exam results, so very long since I have loved anyone but you and longer than that since I was ignorant. Working in the Municipal Library I find it hard to remember, yet harder to forget, how it was that summer.

Sometimes, in these later summers, I pass flower shops full of lilies, or at Easter see them proud upon the altar. In autumn the sycamore across the road sheds big discoloured leaves that start between the cars, slither across the pavement and press wetly against our hall door. Then you come, Aileen, with our yellow handled broom and sweep them out of the gutter, while I stand in the Front Room, watching. So, since you sweep away my tatty leaves, you must bear fardels in their stead. Bear my summer loves, my sweet summer loves. I am not sorry; it is all I have to give you. You, whom I love, working solemnly at your lectures in the drear university, while I catalogue books in the Municipal Library.

'Yet what is love, I pray thee say?
It is but work on holy day.'

Helen

I was constipated with love. Perhaps it is always so in adolescence, I have not read enough of those books to know. I lay awake in my wide, high bed, watching the shadows from the sycamores that guarded the avenue twitch and jiggle across the walls. These were liberally punctuated with Lionel Edwards hunting prints in gross black frames. The horses cavorted in the dancing light. I was still a bit drunk. I was afraid to switch on the bedside light, partly because someone was still awake in the house (I could see a gleam of reflected light and hear a radio playing Chopin downstairs) and partly because the lamp itself buzzed and flickered and had a burn on the shade where a previous guest had tried to cope with it. If he couldn't I saw no reason to assume that I could, so I lay in darkness hoping that the moths would find a way out before they found me. It was very hot. It was the first time in my life that I had been lonely, and I didn't like it. I remember lifting my arms up to find the draught, turning my hands this way and that and saying aloud, in a moment of nightmare premonition, 'O, God, whoever You may be, don't take Lyn away for ever.'

I had thought that all the love there was had gone to Lyn, maybe in that at least I had been right. But I was not thinking of her. I was thinking of Dominic SanFé and his silent face. I can't explain it. I can't be ashamed of it. I can't be objective about it. He was the only man I have ever wanted, and I wanted him for his incredible beauty. If I need any defence at this stage, then this is it, and there is no answer to it. I lay in the shadowy bed, exposed to his beauty like a baby lusting to be tickled.

Downstairs the music stopped. Something slammed. The moon danced in the light streamers of cloud. I think there is always a wind up there on Calary, between the mountains and the sea. I heard it moving among the gross sycamore leaves and heard the sound of footsteps mounting the tall stone staircase, crossing the landing and echoing through my floorboards. Someone in the room below. Diminished in my bed, I knew that there was now only one way to get to sleep. Because even as early as that I knew his footsteps. How else was I supposed to rest with that dark, Cluniac face staining the white linen below me?

I could not even do that.

So, I could not sleep.

▣

'It's only me, miss, Doreen. I've brought you tea, like.' But her hair was the same colour as his, and she was slight and shielded, and nightmare and madness rode high with the high morning sun.

▣

'What are you going to do?' Francis asked Topsy.

'I'm going to art school. In London. It starts at the beginning of October.'

'Where will you live?'

'I've got digs in the Cromwell Road.'

'That'll be noisy,' Francis remarked casually.

Topsy looked snubbed. I thought perhaps she didn't know where the Cromwell Road was, as her parents made her go to and from school by boat. Mother said it was an unnecessary experience for a school-girl, and for once I agreed with her. Stephanie and I both had gone by air.

'Noisy digs will be better than Dublin,' she retorted

crossly. 'Anything would be better than this hole in the mud. Anyone with any go or talent leaves as soon as his parents will let him.'

I thought that if he had any go, he would depart long before that.

'Which have you?' Francis asked her, but he was smiling and she was only slightly upset.

'Both,' she said sharply.

We were sitting on a log at the fringe of the wood. Further in among the trees we could hear the voices of the Seniors and see the drifts of blue smoke curling up from their fire. We couldn't hear what they said but were close enough to hear the tones and inflexions of their grown-up voices saying grown-up things. Topsy and Francis and I had automatically split ourselves off into a Junior group. I was pleased to find that Topsy was unnerved as well as I. Francis was plainly terrified, mostly of Dominic, and subsequently of everyone Dominic took notice of. That made me and Topsy quite safe companions for him. Anna should have been with us, but Maria had captured her and she had left us some time ago, with a nervous smile. We had been sitting together ever since, largely because we didn't know what we were supposed to be doing. Every now and then we looked over our shoulders to make sure that the Seniors were still there. It was very hot. Do you remember how hot it was that summer? I rolled in the leaves, a terrible *grotesquerie* of Lynlessness, drawing her face in my mind but unable to see it. I can't take Dominic without you. I can't. I am ugly and short and fat. I am dull, rather smelly and badly educated. I have not the remotest chance of even catching his eye. So stay with me now. STAY WITH ME NOW. STAY WITH . . . O God how ridiculous I am.

43

Is there no one big enough for me? No one who can beat me at my own game? No one except this Dominic? And that, I realised, rolling over at the sound of his name, was the crux of the problem. I was less stupid than I imagined at times. I knew about hawks and things.

'I was only saying that I went to the same school as Dominic did,' Francis replied when I had said 'What?' 'It's a Jesuit seminary behind St. Pancras Railway Station. The family founded it, or whatever, and we all go there.'

'I can't imagine him at school,' I said slowly, seeing school ties and exercise books and the mysteries of communal baths after rugger that I had heard about.

'Nor could he. Or so they say. I wasn't there then. They say if he hadn't been who he was he'd have been flung out ten times over in a year.' The note of worship crept in surreptitiously. Topsy looked up irritably. 'They say he climbed out every night nearly. He used to go to Soho after women, and the Albert Hall and Covent Garden. In tails. He bicycled right through London in tails every night.'

Francis' gentle eyes were half shut like a mediaeval story teller chanting of the heroes. Is there no one except this Dominic?

'He was caught once by one of the Fathers, in the bicycle shed, with nothing on except an opera hat, singing *The Magic Flute* in the dark, at midnight.'

'Golly,' Topsy said. She had a literal mind. 'Did they expel him?'

'No. He walked out the next term and went somewhere else. I don't know how he dared, just walking out like that. I couldn't.'

'Does he always do just what he likes?' I asked into

the wistful pause. Who hasn't imagined himself just walking out of school?

'I don't know. I don't really know him. I've only seen him at family do's and so on before. But he does what he likes then, all right. And if the uncles or anyone gets cross with him he just grins and goes away. But they say he has an awful temper when he gets roused.'

Just like the heroes. Just like the story books. Just like I had always imagined. He would have stayed on the Salisbury train and taken the bus up along the Avon, through Amesbury and Durrington. To Upavon. Where the harebells were, and Lyn was; I had got no further than Paddington. I felt sick and thought of the chalk and the stunted thorns in the dry valleys. And of Lyn, who also had just walked out. Dear, precious Lyn, what did you have to run away from? And for the first time I thought, or to? Stay with me now . . . now and in the hour of our death . . .

'I'm going to look at Anna's horse,' I said abruptly. 'If l see her I'll ask her if we can ride this afternoon.'

I looked at them. Francis' eyes were shining, and he was picking at the moss with long, idolatrous fingers. Topsy's eyes were shining too, but she was looking at Francis. I couldn't bear them. Through the trees I could hear his voice and my sister's. I turned and wandered away across the lawn, stuffing my hands deep into my pockets like I did with my school blazer to wring this Dominic from my guts.

The back of the house faced north. Part of the area in front of the windows was taken up by a tiny walled-in garden and the rest by the yard. It was into the garden that I now went, through a wrought-iron gate set in the wall and overhung on the outside by wisteria and inside by rambling white roses and their suckers. On my right the dining-room windows leered out through more unpruned Rosaceae, sp. unknown, but too old, too long and too heavy. Instead of passing through and out into the yard through the opposing gate, I turned in along the paving to a little ornamental pool and sat on a slab of polished marble, set as a seat beside the water. Three ivory water-lilies swung on their stalks. Opposite me I could see the back of the great vase of gladioli that had framed his head last night and the back of the black armed chair beyond it. It was an heraldic device without an occupant. I regarded it for some time, dry with sleeplessness and the aftermath of heavy wines. I thought his absence was as formidable as his presence and turned to watch the water-lilies. Do you remember how hot it was that summer? Not a leaf moved in all that disarrayed foliage. For birds only the sleepy, summer pigeon made representation and a bantam clucked. Summer sounds. The griping in the bowels, the sweat behind the knees were summer feelings. Last summer's too. For Lyn. I thought of her in her blue coat and skirt, and flat blue hat, as I had last seen her walking out of the drive in front of the Seniors' Door to be driven to Swindon station in Matron's old Ford. The limes had been flaccid with perfume, the gravel dusty. I had been thirsty then, too. The gate in the yard wall squealed. I looked up in fear. The French woman came in. She was carrying a cardboard box of lettuces and radishes. A cucumber keeled over in one corner. The leaves were touched with dry, yellowy sand. She saw me, saw me watching her with Lyn stark in my face, and came up to the marble bench.

'It is too hot for crying,' she said abruptly. Her tone startled me, but I could not look up. She stood over me, her breasts above my head. 'Such desolation is unbecoming in a rose garden. For whom are you crying?' When I did not answer she said peremptorily, 'One always cries for someone, if only for oneself.'

And I was afraid of her, as she might be a powerful tutor, and I unable to comprehend. 'For a girl,' I said at last and without humility. She put the lettuces between our feet and sat on the bench with me. I remember that I did not move along. 'Older than me, you know? That's all.'

'I know,' she said.

There was a message in her eyes when she turned to look at me, but it was very largely written, and I could not get it all in focus. We were sitting very close together. In my tummy something fluttered and I drew back defensively from it. Mistaking the gesture, she moved along the bench, stooping to thrust the cucumber more securely into the box. It flashed across my mind that she blushed a little, and my insides quivered again. 'How old are you?' I asked suddenly, shocking myself. There were fine lines about her mouth, but no hairs.

'I am thirty-nine. Next month I will be forty. That is older than you.'

I stared at her. Carefully I watched her bony hand come out and rest upon mine like a winged creature, settle and dart away.

'I am twenty years too old to be unhappy.'

'That's longer than I have been alive,' I said wonderingly. 'You were crying when I was being born?'

'Most certainly I was. When you were born I was in my twenties, and I stopped crying for good.'

She did not look at me again but rose and walked quickly from the garden, carrying her box upon her hip.

She had very long thighs like a man's, or a dancer's. Like Dominic's. For a long time I sat and stared at the water. Her French accent was more pronounced than his and more easily defined. It gave importance to her words—but she had not said much. I stretched out behind me and pulled off a rose, struggling a little with the stem. It did not prick me. I laid it on the seat when I got up and left it there in the garish sunlight.

Once or twice I thought, O God, but aimlessly and out of habit. The garden and the exchange had had an anodyne effect. I felt nothing at all except the lassitude of sleeplessness and found it a comfortable condition.

I did not hear the stable clock strike eleven. For some time I wandered about the little garden. It had a reserved quiet which put me in mind of nuns and the silence of the cloisters. I thought of the blinkers on the wimples and how many terrible sights they must exclude, turning the eyes forever to the front, forever to face forward what was coming immediately ahead. Head on to God, head on to myself. There did not seem then to be anything immediate in the idea of being head on to God, but the other was not a subject for the squeamish. I think that in those days I had so little understanding of what it was all about that I still believed in some remote part of my body, that one day I would turn into a man. When that happened, it would be all right. I remember the very calm feeling of the belief—the certainty, the simplicity of it. It was an idea as pure as the veil, as quiet as the habit, as exotic as the Rosary. It was what I was all about. The corporeal fact that people saluted and called 'Helen' would go away. I would be as I was. As, perhaps, I am. There had been no more to it, until Lyn. I had had crushes before and have had them since. I know the difference.

It was love. Irremediable love. With no redress. For it was my flesh that stirred for her. Round and round the roseberry bush, in and out the lilies, that's the way the craving goes. Pop. Pop indeed. For now I had to face Dominic. And Dominic was beautiful. Dominic was strong. Dominic was altogether everything I had thought he was when I saw him as an Iron Angel come to scorch me with the fires of hell, harrowing Brown Thomas' coffee room at eleven in the morning. And I did not know whether to pray that Dominic might rescue me from Lyn, or that Lyn should save me from Dominic. So I paced around the three still lilies wondering how long the tenuous links between body and mind would last. It was very hot that summer. Yet the French ballerina had been cool enough . . . The lilies were cool enough.

I thought that such loving and such grief must mark me. I leaned over the pool as if to see my reflection. It is a measure of my duplicity that I did not know whom I was expecting to see. The sun was high and I saw no reflection. I was not surprised, but I was saddened beyond bearing. There was none to help me. Not even our brother the Water, who at least was clean. I remember standing there for a long time in the sun, while the rose on the marble opened a little and began to die. It was a measure of my duplicity that I followed where the French woman had gone and remembered how long her thighs were, with the cold guilt of a recovering lover.

◻

Inside the house I met Anna. She was coming out of her mother's room on the first floor as I turned across the landing to go up the next flight of stairs to my room.

In the shadow of the door she was small and very unafraid. Her tiny voice was clear in the high spaces of the house. 'I will hate you for this as long as I live,' she called over her shoulder.

Behind her Maria's harsh tenor shouted, 'Grow up, before I put a fire under your pale little skirts!' and her crackling laughter stopped at the shutting of the door.

Shocked we looked at each other. It was Anna who said 'I'm sorry,' and made as if to move past me.

I said, 'I'm sorry. I didn't hear you . . . ' and fumbled for the bannister.

It seemed too high a price for a collection of Lalique glass.

Anna looked at me in the dusty sunlight, coming slowly from the door. If she were embarrassed it was on my behalf. Her eyes were half closed against the light. Her mouth was very small and perfect. She said, 'Some of my mother's plans are not very nice.'

I turned frantically for the stair. I did not want to see her cry. But I heard the harsh sound of it as she went down and I up. I thought of the dark stain of his head on her pillows every night and of her white hands, and I felt sick. I thought that Anna was very grown-up indeed, and that I was very smutty, and what the hell was the use of wanting to be a man, when you didn't even know what it was like to be kissed by one, let alone what one looked like with nothing on? And my hands performed ritual motions and reminiscent flutterings until I caught sight of myself in the mirror and was shamed out of all proportion to my guilt, because at the same time I heard his voice on the terrace below, and his image made my flesh crawl and sweat leap out in great globules of lust up and down my bottom and between my legs and I was the filthiest thing in the whole of that rotten, degenerate house. I got up and pulled the bed together, lest Doreen should know what I had been doing, and was humiliated by the necessity of dry knickers and not knowing where to wash the blue ones . . .

Then I saw him. He was going into the library in front of me. For whole seconds I watched his back, and no one could see my face. Even now when I think of him it is his back that I see first. I think I had never seen a man's back before, nor have seen another since. It had that rare beauty of a voice proclaiming 'April.'

I am not naturally gregarious. When they all suggested swimming as a way of passing the afternoon, I was horrified. The thought of exposing my body in a busty, red bathing dress was anathema. It had nylon nets for the breasts to dangle in, making them prickly and itchy in the cold water, and what seemed to be acres of featureless belly surface for drops to hover and splat on. It mortified me to think that Topsy and the French woman would see me thus. But the only valid excuse was unthinkable and thinking it made me blush so that my hands did their familiar sausage impersonation and I dropped my cigarette. I was taking this smoking seriously. It suited me. I had made the movements so often and was so familiar with the classic gesture of lighting and tapping that I don't think I ever looked gauche with a cigarette, not even the first time. There were a few intimate details to be worked out, of course, like talking with one in your mouth, or, as in this case, wanting to get at your hanky with a sherry glass in the other hand.

We were having ritualistic pre-luncheon drinks in the library. Nothing but whiskey or sherry. I doubted if there was anything but whiskey or sherry, ever. I knew that Stephanie liked gin and wondered how she was faring. She was faring nicely with whiskey and Dominic. I homed in comfortably behind Matthew Frost with my spine to Matthew Arnold and my left shoulder pressed up against Hoare's *History of Wexford* in six volumes. It was a comfortable enough niche from which to watch, while I worked out a way of avoiding indecent exposure on the shingle at Killiney. But I couldn't take my eyes from Dominic. His hair was the colour of worn saddlery, and he seemed ephemeral. It may have been the sherry or the sound of Arnold's ignorant armies in my nervous column that made the scene like something from an opera. At any moment I expected everyone to burst into arpeggios about the table being laid and the curtains to sweep in between them and me. But the only curtains in the room were long, rusty velvet things on either side of the windows, and the air of transcience was permanent. Like the principal tenor Dominic took centre stage, slight as one who might die soon, perhaps in the second act. The cast grouped about him, all solo parts. There were a lot of solo parts. I had not thought before that they were all solo parts. All principals. I had seen them as existing to particularise him—Stephanie to accentuate his sensuality, Francis to give substance to his strength like glass in stone arches. I had come to watch a melodrama and would be restive until it began. I alone was the audience, I, in my myriad facets, sitting back in the dark, watching. Then I remembered the sound Anna had made on the stairs, and the ache in my belly at the sight of the French woman's back in the stone rose-garden;

I felt the touch of his hand as he took me off the floor after the Charleston, a week ago. I thought, I will not go on stage with them. I will not. And thought that, really, I need not. And furthermore, please bear in mind that I was very young, and had never seen a comic opera in my life.

It was decided that we should ride to the sea. It was a long way, six or seven miles, but across the bog, under the shoulder of the mountain, and down narrow stony lanes. There was some problem about horses; there were five in the place. Eventually Maria took it upon herself to organise the matter. She did it in a singular way.

'Carracas is a valuable hunter,' she announced. "Therefore Anna will ride him. You won't do him too much harm if you don't interfere with him. Laurence, you will obviously ride your own. You don't want her mucked up at this stage. Helen can therefore ride Shirley—that's Anna's. Quite simple, but don't nag at her. Then there is only old Trottomina left. Topsy, you're not very good, are you? But I suppose you can manage her; she's nearly twenty-two, and if you fall off it's not far from the ground.' She stood back complacently as if she'd done something nice for us all. Then her eye caught Dominic's. His eyebrow was twitching. She scowled at him. In the silence in which I was expecting her to offer him a dun cow or a St. Bernard dog for a treat, Anna said in a curiously high, atonal voice, 'Loftus. He can take Loftus to the sea.'

Dominic's eyebrow steadied, then lifted. He looked at Anna. 'Why Loftus?'

'His legs need the sea-water,' she replied in the same dreamy, monotonous voice.

I saw Matthew put a hand on her arm. She said nothing more. Everyone was very quiet, stilled by her tone.

53

'Maria,' the French woman said firmly.

'Yes, Laurence?' Maria was staring at Anna, and Anna stared back.

'Maria, Dominic is too light for Loftus. He could get hurt.'

Maria glanced at her, dismissively, nodded a couple of times and observed. 'The devil looks after his own. Lunch ready yet, Grogan?'

As she turned to lead us from the library, Dominic put his hand out and caught her above the elbow. She stopped, drawn close to him. His hands were shockingly strong. Their faces nearly met. They were very alike. In a slurred voice she said, 'Gerald was always a good rider. Even a fool respected Gerald on a horse.'

'I am not Gerald,' he spat at her, savagely.

I think we all became a little frightened. I think his eyes opened a little. His body shook. 'Gerald, Gerald! Mean bastards, the pair of you, mean bastards—' she shouted into his face. He caught her shoulders, shaking the old woman a little, and cried out, 'Bloody Gerald. Gerald is dead, remember? I buried him. Locked the crypt gate on him! I am not Gerald and I will not be impaled on him . . . he's dead.'

'Doesn't seem to have made a farthing's worth of difference,' she muttered, looking at his hands on her arms. Gloomily she put an old woman's fingers on his bright hair. 'Not here, anyway. Come and carve the lamb for me.'

He sighed a little and offered her his arm, drawing her from the room in front of us all, deep lines appearing beside his mouth that I had not seen before.

In a frenzy I thought, He's not an angel—he's real. There was a seagull calling out over the garden as I followed Topsy from the room.

'You must forgive me,' he said, crossly, stooping over the carving table behind Maria's back, 'but this creature has a most outrageous anatomy. Is there a smaller knife, Grogan?'

'It broke its leg on Kippure. East face,' Maria informed him over her shoulder.

'My God. Does it matter which face of the flipping mountain it broke its leg on?'

'It's full of little channels under the heather,' Maria went on, 'and it may not have quite got the geography of the place.'

'Evidently not.'

'Or it may have fallen off a rock.'

'Possibly.'

' . . . in the rain.'

'Damn it, Maria, I couldn't care less how the silly thing sprained its ankle, or whatever it did. The point is that I can't carve it.'

He glared at her over his hunched shoulders, baleful, mean, stammering. He took another knife held out by. Grogan. 'Thanks. Anyway, mountain sheep don't sprain their legs on a bit of heather in a drizzle. I bet you shot it, or snared it, or found the carcass or something.'

He was about to laugh when Maria, quite close to him, leaned her chair back on its hind legs and said, 'It wasn't a mountain sheep. It was a Suffolk.'

'A SUFFOLK?'

'Yes. I bought a small flock last year. Very expensive . . .'

'Mother of God—you're not trying to breed Suffolks on the East face of where-ever—? Are you?'

He spun round from the table and stood over her, a knife dripping fat held at arm's length behind her.

'Don't get so jiggy, Dominic. Susannah told me when I was there last year that she had great success with hers.'

'Maria. You spent one night with Aunt on your way up to town. You may not have noticed either that she is completely gaga or that she lives in Monmouthshire. Aunt sold her sheep thirty years ago, at a loss, and even then they were pastured in nice fat land. At the moment I have some sheep on her land, and they are not Suffolks. The Suffolks are in Somerset.'

'Do put that knife down, Dominic.'

Harriet started to giggle. Relieved we all looked at her.

Bill said, 'Ssh! I want to hear the next instalment of the Suffolk Saga.'

'You have never seen Laurie's aunt. Have you met her, Francis?'

'Yes, in Somerset.' And he started to giggle too, despite Dominic growling in the background. 'She was dressed as a brigand, and she had a Russian maid who refused to speak English or French and wore real pearls when she brought up the early morning tea. I thought she was super.'

'The maid or the aunt?' Matthew asked, deeply interested.

'If it wasn't for old Olga, either you, Maria, or your father, Francis, or I would have to look after Aunt, so just keep civil about her.'

'Sorry, Dominic.' He blushed and stared at his knife. Dominic grunted at him and Maria said nervously, 'Why me?'

'Because now that Kate is dead, you are one of the senior females. I couldn't cope with Aunt and Olga. I don't speak Russian, to start with, and Aunt thinks I'm Gerald, and Olga thinks I'm Aunt's illegitimate son.'

'Does she really, why?' Even Anna was getting interested now. This seemed to strike her as especially funny, and she laughed at him, mocking him for something. 'That's lovely, isn't it, Ma?'

'Anna, do be quiet.' Maria was really nervous, now, glancing at Dominic who had turned his attention back to the lamb. 'Topsy, do take some peas. They're out of the garden.'

'Remember to spit out the pips, Topsy,' Dominic murmured.

'PIPS?'

'Special variety imported from Senegal in 1372, and only grown here. Very profitable export trade with the Esquimaux colony in Manchester. That's how Maria makes her money, isn't it, love?'

'Dominic, do get off my back, dear.' Maria sounded annoyed. Topsy looked doubtfully at her plate. 'Topsy, don't be silly. They are perfectly ordinary peas.'

Matthew laughed inordinately. 'There was ceiling plaster in my sugar this morning,' he announced gleefully. 'I'd watch it, Topsy.'

Topsy, aware of having been teased, flushed and ate peas with much hauteur. I hugged my pleasure in her discomfort.

Dominic's ill-temper broke, and he started to laugh too. 'You're lucky to have any plaster on your ceiling, Matthew. There is one island left on the north-east of mine. I estimate it at six inches square, and with a life span of another twenty-four hours. It's exactly over the mirror. But as I am evidently to be prematurely slaughtered by the mighty Loftus this afternoon, there is little cause for worry.' He brought his own plate down the table and sat in his chair. So that was what was riling him. I wondered if he were afraid. 'May I borrow a hard hat, Maria, or is that unsporting?' She ignored him.

▣

'Laurie, Laurie—wait a minute—' Harriet was running across the yard, and he reined in beside her, leaning from the saddle, puzzled.

'What's the matter? No, don't come too close.'

'Just, oh, nothing, just to take care.' Her long face was harrowed looking. He frowned in evident distress.

'Don't be silly, lovey. I'm very careful. Look, I have a hat and all.' He smiled, but it was serious.

Only because I was directly behind I heard her say, 'I can't do without you. Please take care.' And he muttered, 'You're going to have to, sweet. But I think not yet.' And he touched her chin with the whip. 'Keep away, now, this is a beastly creature. Don't forget to bring my things in the car with yours. They're in my room, somewhere. Try the towel rail.'

He nudged at the gaunt horse, and Loftus swung slightly. Harriet watched us leave the yard. I could see no danger, but all the little lines around her eyes were strong in the sunlight.

I had been impressed by his caution. He had checked everything that could be checked on the saddlery. He came last, behind us all. He was much too light. It was hot, and flies tickled and stung as we meandered under the sycamores and through the rhododendrons. Topsy was unhappy on the old pony and kept kicking at its fat, hairy sides, which seemed to make it unhappy, too. Anna kept glancing back at Dominic. So did I. So did the French woman, who came up beside me. 'Shirley and Arras like each other,' she explained as the horses rubbed their cheeks on each other's bridles. Our boots touched, swung away, touched again. Dominic rode with both reins in one hand, like a polo player, or a huntsman. I let the arm beside the French woman dangle. Now and again her knee brushed it. It was very hot. We came out on to the road, left it for the bog, and the trails of coarse grass between the gorse bushes and the spreads of heather.

I said at last, 'What is your name?'

'How lovely that you do not yet know!' She laughed, showing me white even teeth and a rippling in her throat, which was not smooth like ours, nor wrinkled like Maria's, but somewhere between the two. 'It is the same as his,' she jerked her head back at Dominic. 'Laurence. Spelt the way you would spell it for a man. The same exactly.' She smiled at me, enigmatic in the glare and the swaying of the horses. 'We are cousins of a sort. All of us.' A fly lit on the corner of her mouth, and she blew at it. The sea glittered over the brow of the hill.

'Why do they call him Dominic, then?' I asked, softly.

'Oh, it's half a title and part of his name. It's a tradition. All the SanFés call him Dominic, except the old aunt, I think. And the people here call him the Dominic, using it like a title. I don't know if they do in England.'

It sounded rather feudal to me. 'Harriet calls him Laurie,' I said, remembering.

'Harriet is his foster-sister, her family brought him up, I think. So does Bill. They were at university together.'

That cleared up that temporary muddle. 'Who are you?' I wanted to know now.

'I am not anyone, except where other people make me into a curiosity.'

I felt like Topsy had looked with her pip-infested peas. The horses had drawn apart wiggling their hind quarters as we went down a steep lane. I thought it was time we talked about horses. I could hear the slither and rattle of Loftus skittering around the ruts and stones. I was

59

herded by him behind me. I was harrassed and hurried by his being there just behind me. He had said nothing, had never come up from the back. I had not dared to turn too often, to see. 'What's wrong with Loftus?'

'He is vicious, and when he has you on the ground he puts his feet on you and stamps.' She made a monstrous gesture, and I shivered as we passed under a cluster of elderberries.

'Why doesn't Lady Calary sell him?'

'No one will buy him.'

She looked at me in the sun. She had a white scarf around her hair, and I could see thin little collar bones under her shirt. Our boots brushed and fell apart again without sensation.

The others had arrived before us. They were standing on the shingle in their swimming things. They were all very tall. Anna was at the end of the row, tiny on the tall grey horse. Mutely we lined up behind the semi-naked figures. The waves rustled the razor-shells. The sea went on till it got to England, where Lyn was. I thought Stephanie looked silly in mauve, undressed, while we sweated in boots and twill. They were looking at a dead jelly-fish. It had colours like Mother's pheasant feathers deep down in itself. They were wondering if it stung. If there were others. Francis said no, and they accepted it because his father was an Admiral. Higher up in the white dry sand Dominic was cagily walking Loftus in small circles. He rode with his hands curiously far apart, like one is told not to, so that the horse seemed suspended from him rather than supporting him. I thought it had the biggest teeth I had ever seen outside the zoo. And the dirtiest. We tied up the horses except for Loftus, whom they penned in a corner of the field, parking the cars on each side of him, and pulling an old bedstead across the space between the bonnets. Dominic said it was crazy, that he'd jump out and smash the windscreens. The others disagreed, and he turned away with a shrug. I suddenly saw the streaks of sweat down the lines beside his mouth and the glistening around his throat. Six miles in the sun, on that brute.

He sat heavily in the sun, sand clinging to the damp patches around his shoulders. 'Matthew, tug my boots, be a comfortable fellow.' He lay back and waggled his foot in the air, his hat over his eyes. Matthew complied, and tickled his soles. Dominic shrieked most unheroically and writhed in the sand, rolling and yelling and kicking at Matthew, whose phenomenal length kept him well out of range. Dominic was nearly in tears, when he got free, struggling to his feet like a sand-creature made by bored children, shouting, 'You rotten bastard. You mean, deceitful, BIG bastard!' and he hurled his hat at Matthew, who hopped out of the way and turned slowly to watch it spinning out to the edge of the waves.

A pair of solemn children they watched it spin to the water, slither with a faery notion of spray on to the wave top, dither in the crest and slip back into the trough behind. In a flurry of paste glitter the sun picked out the passage of the brim. The tide was going out. Wondering, too, I watched the sea take away this new creature, unquestioning, unmotivated.

'Jesu, mercy!' Dominic's hand covered his mouth and his eyes turned helplessly to Harriet. 'It's Maria's hat.'

The beginning of a harsh laugh broke from the French woman's lips. 'Jesu, mercy!' she mimicked, as Harriet started running into the water.

Dominic hesitated and suddenly ran after her. The

bowler had not gone far. I saw him plunge full length at it, his arms tearing at the water, great silky floods of it washing over his shirt and shoulders all dark and colourless in the sun. He stood up, breast deep in the sea, laughing in the sun, riotous, pointless laughter. Ha ha! in the sun. Ha ha ha in the very bright sun. Fifteen, twenty pounds worth of breeches sodden in sea, ha ha, and a soggy brim to the hat. The sun blazed, the sea danced, mindlessly as laughter. I turned away up the beach and sat in the ploughed-up marks he had made. I knew that no one would notice.

Indifferently I changed behind the hedge into my shaming costume. I swam in the sea. I listened to them tease and chatter. I saw him half-naked in white sharkskin, lying dripping on a towel, a cigarette pungent and sweet between his sweet lips. I put my head down and lay in the dark below the sun, warm, wet, like a private, interior agony. I had not thought to hear him laugh. He did not look like one who laughed. I could not laugh and saw that the difference between us was not one of anything but the ability to laugh. I had thought the only bond between us to be the blank between his eyes and the world and saw that this could be shrouded over with laughter, and I left mourning a hidden thing. The heat made me sleepy, the hissing of the little waves drew off down the sands. I looked up into the wild white sand, tossed by bodies, the shells scattered, the drift disorganised out of its placid arrangement. I looked over my shoulder. Matthew and Anna were away down by the sea, withdrawn in a quiet seclusion of distance. Topsy and Francis were up by the cars with the French woman, Topsy idly holding out bits of coarse grass to Loftus, whose head was swinging about irritably to avoid her. I thought, silly fool, she'll annoy him. I was aware of the fact that Dominic was a long way off; I looked and could not see him. It had come to that stage, that private stage when the eyes are a desirable accessory, no more. It has come to that, I thought. The body knew he was not there. That was love of a kind—the body knowing, not needing to be told, when it itself was not even concerned. The brain, the dark mind quivering away, a labouring of the senses that left a whole evolutionary phase behind. The body, I thought, the body . . . which body . . . whose body, I thought, I do not know this body of mine that tells me he is not within sight. I must check up, scientifically search the beach, verify what this dark, recessed body tells me. I must not believe it implicitly it is only the body. Love is an exalted thing, a thing of total belief and total annihilation, such as I knew for Lyn. And total pain, captured and held close, lest it surge out and overwhelm, thus annihilating even its own extinguishing force. Love is a *not* thing. This new little pain is something quite other, a new and unlovely knowledge that I do not need, will never need. Go away, little pain, hop out there into the sun and die of the emptiness in the shingle. Go away. I could not hold this new pain dear, could not embrace it and be clutched by it, as I had the older pain. In its sharp smallness it was alien and strange, and I could not live with it. His beauty nibbling at the vital parts of my ugly little frame. God be with all those who love in the summer time. God it was who had said let there be light and had thoughtlessly provoked this blank stare that we call the sun. No sense of privacy, the deity. I rolled over on my back and stared at Harriet. Bill had his hand lightly on her belly, just below the waist. Stephanie was combing her hair, thin strands clinging to her salty neck and some to the comb. She no longer looked silly in mauve, half undressed, but vulnerable like the body of exposed mollusca, raw, violet, damp in the dry poisonous air. I wondered for a fleeting second if she had some little pain somewhere that made her lips full and bitten-looking like that.

'I hope he gets lost,' Bill muttered.

'Who?' Harriet peered down over her sharp breasts at his face beside her waist.

'Laurie.'

'WHY?'

'Because it would be nice to have an evening out with you, without him peering over my shoulder all the time. Jealous bastard.'

'He's not jealous. He's protective. There is nothing in it for him.' She spoke softly, her hand making a sketch of a caress in the sand by his shoulder.

'Isn't there?' He watched her hand, myopically attentive to its burrowing by him in the disarrayed sand.

I wondered how they had not noticed him. How they could not have seen him, even, long ago. He dropped down beside her, brushing sand off his feet. They were long and narrow. He was watching Bill. 'No,' he answered for her. 'Though I would have it otherwise.' He reached out and pulled her head round to him, tugging at her hair. 'Isn't that so, love?' The fear-lines leaped about her eyes.

'Shut up, Laurie,' she said, compliant in his grasp. It was Bill's turn to watch, and mine, and Stephanie's. No sense of privacy in their eyes, no shame in the slight stir in the sand. His lips moved but no sound came. She looked away to Bill's hand by her. Beggared of her eyes he looked at Bill, too. 'See?' he said lightly.

64

'Helen, are you riding back?'

Aghast, I turned to Stephanie. She was looking pointedly at her watch. I stumbled to my feet, rearing my bottom up backwards like a cow, because I had been lying on my face. With my buttocks in mid-air and my hair stinging my left eyeball, I replied, 'No.' A thought struck me. I flattened out again and put my head in the sand. 'No, Peter is riding Shirley back. Francis is taking Trottomina, Topsy—'

I couldn't see her look, but I could feel it. I thought ostriches were quite the cleverest birds on record. After all, she couldn't see me feeling it . . . I could feel my breasts oozing out of their little nylon bags. O God, I couldn't get up now anyway, lest they flop out altogether. I suddenly had a passionate urge to get up and run away. I had been eavesdropping. I remembered an occasion at school when the biology mistress had caught me turning over to the chapter on reproduction, when she was talking about photosynthesis. I had had to tell the class what I was looking at . . . 'Hips,' I had said in a lordly fashion. 'Mine are too big.' I got the laugh, but I lost the round, and the biology mistress knew it. I wriggled back a fraction, squashing the red linen upwards against the sand. The mammaries moved implacably ahead of their containers. Perhaps if I wiggled forwards . . . ? O, God, shove the bloody buz back where it belongs . . . please, DEAR God . . . I should have known better than to lie on my face in the first place. Nonchalantly I whistled the first bars of the Funeral March. They vanished into the sand. So did my lips. I spat.

'Helen!'

'Stephanie,' I said firmly. 'You have a lack of appreciation of other people's physical circumstances which is positively feline.'

It was Dominic's snort of laughter that brought me to my feet. Facing the sea I fled from them, running in a great circle, stuffing my top down, and hoping I was too far away to be observed. Pat-patty-pat on the wet sand, while my agony subsided. I ran out of breath. I walked slowly away in my dirty costume, grey and smeared. 1 had lost that round, too. Dumbly I joined up with Topsy, Francis and the French woman.

Peter came out from behind the hedge where he had apparently been changing. He was immaculate in the sort of shirt that is made out of the material one uses for horse-rugs, white and floppy with yellow and brown squares. I glared at him with hatred. His hair was damp and curly. He looked like the Glass Industry going riding during a house-party. Partly because I had a stitch, and partly because I didn't want to look at his plump, spanielly face, I leaned over the mud-guard of the car where there was a great batch of sorrel.

It was dry and dead, the seeds almost black on the tall stalks. It was the red colour of the hair above Dominic's ears. The car wheel had run over part of the patch, and it leaned out like broken old bones. There were five stalks upright. I was counting the broken ones . . .

◉

The noise was appalling. Topsy screaming, Peter shouting, the shriek of metals tearing each other, and above all the din of the iron shod hooves flailing in hysteria, thud thud thud thud thud, as Loftus fought the bedstead out of the bumpers, lashed at the car bonnet, reared till his pale belly was black against the sun . . . Huge hooves how close, how vastly hard above; little

flecks of whipped spittle and grass on my eyes; the
French woman hitting my head away and grabbing
pointlessly at the reins slipping through her fingers.
Blood now on the sorrel, and the sound of Dominic's
voice calling us to leave him, for Christ's sake, alone.
Thudding in my head and armpits where the fear was. He
is nearly here, I could not watch the blue hooves strike
at him, heard only his breath, knew it was his, heard the
tiny squeak of leather on sweaty hands. Her hands gripped
me round the upper arms. I could feel her ribs quivering.
I pressed back into her, watching Dominic and the horse,
and the bedstead caught in the reins. The sun flashed on
the old brass knobs. Peter moved forward uncertainly
and then started to run, Matthew and Bill catching up
as they tumbled up off the sand on to the curt, sharp
grass. Loftus was heading down towards them, dragging
Dominic and the bedstead with him, kicking indiscriminately at both. Dominic had one hand up near his head,
the other spread out along his back, twisted in the end of
the stirrup leathers. The bedstead banged at his bare
legs, the horse's hooves stamped within a fraction of his
feet. She was muttering in French in her throat; I could
feel it reverberating against me. The saddle began to slip,
Dominic's purchase on the leathers loosening as his own
weight pulled the saddle round towards him. I heard him
shouting at Matthew to hold the bedstead and saw
Matthew's enormous strength grip and haul on the
flashing brass. Loftus squealed and lashed; the rein
dragged round.

All the time Topsy was crying and the three men were
swinging their weight on the brass, and the sun blared
and glared down on the sand, taking up their shouting
and the thudding and the clanging of metal, and Francis

saying insistently, 'Shut up, Topsy, oh, do shut up, please . . . ' And above his voice Dominic's screaming, 'Harry, Harry, Harry, Bill—' because Harriet was standing in the way, quite still, very small in the sand, her hands clasped up to her lips. Stephanie was running forward to her, and I had a shocked thought—Stephanie is brave, actually brave. But Bill got there faster, and I saw nothing for a second for seeing Stephanie left and the horse running her down, which was not real, for the sand gave grip to Matthew and Peter. And the reins broke, and it was only Dominic and the horse now, free and fast, going for the sea, leaving the terrible metal half-held in Matthew's hands, glinting in the sun, and Bill holding Harriet against his chest and Peter walking slowly towards Stephanie, his hands out, and where was Anna? The girth broke, and the saddle lay upside down in the sand.

It was cold on my arms where she let go of me. There was nothing to do but watch leisurely in the sun. Loftus ran deep into the water, until it slowed him, and Dominic swung himself up on to his bare back, grasping the single rein in one hand and his mane in the other. After a long time going round and round in the water, churning up the dark sand, they came out. The horse was docile, dripping, his head stretched out as if he would suck from the sand. They walked in small circles, round and round and round under the sun, gyrating up the beach to the grass edge. Peter picked up the saddle, the broken girth trailing, and came slowly up to us. Stephanie walked behind him, her eyes down on the grass. Another sorrel stalk snapped as the French woman moved, and I looked at her moving. Her cheeks were scarlet, and her eyes wide and wild. Her lips were parted, and she panted slightly. I sat heavily on the torn bumper. Seagulls screeched over us. The other horses fidgeted and tossed about, watching, Arras quivering, her eyes ringed with white. Anna was stroking Shirley, running her hands over her brow and ears. Matthew was still standing in the sand, holding the knobs of the brass bedstead.

'Laurence, can you come?' She moved quietly towards them. Dominic slid off, gently sidling along Loftus' neck, to hand her the single rein. They spoke slowly in French for a moment, and she walked apart with the horse, still leading it round and round in circles. I wondered why he had selected her, slight and female as she was. He took his clothes from the car and went behind the hedge with them. His feet left specks of blood on the grass, and the backs of his legs were pulpy and dark looking. He walked stiffly, speaking to no one. Matthew moved at last, bringing his boots up to the car. Dominic flung his once-white trunks into the back, took the boots, and put his hand on Matthew's shoulder to steady himself. When he came to the pulpy part of his calves he hesitated for a second and Matthew looked at him. It took ages to get everyone changed, mounted, ready. No one talked much except Topsy, who was shaking so much that she couldn't do up her bra, and Peter, who was dotting about being helpful in all directions. I think he would have done Topsy's hooks and eyes if I had not done them first.

They must have come back very slowly, for we had been hanging about in the avenue for half an hour longer than we expected before we saw the tops of their heads and heard the rattle of hooves on the gravel. The broken saddle leaned drunkenly in the yard, its flaps wide, exposing itself to the evening. Maria had not appeared since we came back. We told the groom what had happened, and how Dominic had slowed the horse and held him in the sea.

'He's a clever hand with the horses. Just like his father, Lord Gerald, that's dead now. And the same to look at too, even mounted. And that's a strange thing, for it's seldom two men ride alike, however they may look. But he's too light for that Loftus, and I don't know what possessed her Ladyship to put him up at all. Still and all, he should have known better than to leave the horse penned up like that, that was a madness.'

I told him how Dominic had been over-ruled on this point and blushed when I saw Matthew's close attention to my defence of him.

The groom laughed. 'Never mind, miss,' he said, 'he'll pay for it riding that Loftus up the mountain with one rein and no saddle. Not that he's not well able for him; they'd be a grand pair now, if they could teach each other sense.' And he laughed again and went to wait in the shadowy saddle room, whistling *Lily Marlene* between his teeth.

Outraged, I stood under the sycamores and went into the library when I saw that they had all come back and that Dominic was still up on Loftus' narrow, rubbed back. He took ages to come in, darkening the door when he did, and a thrill of horror rushed up through my belly. His shirt and breeches were black with bog water, his shirt ripped under the arm, showing the flesh. He limped slightly, and his eyes were as black as pitch. He came through the french doors and went straight to the table where the drinks were. He poured a large Irish whiskey, added nothing to it, and took it to the piano stool, where he sat heavily, cradling it against his thighs.

We were all staring at him, searching for something to say like, well done, or, thanks, or, are you all right, when Maria walked in. He looked up at her, out of his black eyes. She looked down at him. She peered into his glass. His lips began to twitch.

'That's whiskey!' she cried horrified.

'Yes.'

She took it out of his hand, put it on the shelf containing the mediaeval mystics and ethnology and went without a word from the room. Dominic got laboriously to his feet, took the glass, drained it, spluttered, replaced it carefully in front of the *Little Flowers* and was sitting on the stool, still in total silence, when Maria re-entered. Solicitously she handed him a great balloon glass. 'Brendan told me what happened,' she said gruffly.

Dominic put his nose to the glass, quivered, and looked up. 'That's brandy!' he mimicked.

'Gerald always said—'

And he started to laugh, wiping his face with the back of his hand, smearing whiskey and mud and sweat about his cheeks, till it seemed that he was almost crying and not laughing at all, and Matthew took him by the arm, shaking him slightly and saying, 'You're filthy, you need a bath,' and lured him from the room, carrying the brandy in his other hand. As they went out, we heard him say, 'Christ, Matthew, I've never been so frightened for so long in my life!' and his laugh grew quieter as Matthew replied and their footsteps went away.

'He DRANK it!' Maria yelped, gazing at the empty glass in front of the *Little Flowers*. 'And taken the brandy, too.'

It was monstrously last year's. It was yellow with a huge brown velvet chunk that was supposed to accentuate the bosom and yet conceal it. It accentuated mine all right by dint of revealing it to anyone over three foot nine inches tall. Dangling from the lower edge of the velvet was a fringe of gold and yellow beads. Originally I had rather liked these, and last year I had spent many soothing moments at private dances stroking them and making them wave about. As a result there were bald patches now, with the pale and far-from-clean string showing.

I stood up restlessly and wandered over to the dressing table, which in fact was a sideboard and still had a knife sharpener in one of the drawers. I wondered if I should give it to Doreen, in case she was looking for it, but I was frightened of Doreen so I had done nothing about it. Doreen did my room. She was bright and frisky and had knowing little eyes that took in all my morning miseries and my tense, evening shame. Also, I thought she looked remarkably like Maria, and I had noticed too that she had Dominic's long hands, and feet in the tight black lace-ups. Her hair was of their colour, reddish like sorrel. I strongly suspected that she was Maria's child and I had spent some time trying to do sums to see if Maria could have been old enough, or Doreen young enough, and decided that it was easily possible. I was very excited and rather shocked by this and wondered how Anna felt about having her elder half-sister to wash her underwear. It seemed terribly romantic somehow, except, I thought, perhaps for Doreen. I pushed the knife sharpener aside and burrowed under the *Irish Times* which lined the drawer. There was my photo of Dominic. I stared at it for a long time, and then I thought of the dance we were going to tonight, and wondered how I could stand watching Stephanie flirt with him and how, maybe, he would ask me to dance, for duty's sake, and how I would draw myself up and refuse, saying that I was engaged, or occupied, or reserved, like a cafe table, in Brown Thomas' coffee room, and I was thinking when the door opened and Stephanie walked in without knocking, as she always did.

'Can I come in?' she asked, shutting the door firmly behind her, and I laddered my stocking in my haste to scramble away from the side-board. 'Never mind,' she went on, 'it won't show.'

'But you made me do it!'

'Did I really? I'm so sorry. I'll pay you back some time.'

I thought that some time, some long long time away when it was all all right, I would be the one who would do the paying back; then I remembered that she had been confusingly brave this afternoon, and I looked at her owlishly. Maybe she was grown up or something.

'What do you want?' I asked churlishly.

What she really wanted was to find out if the door between our rooms had a key on my side, but it took her an extraordinary length of time to do it. I watched her manœuvering, and she watched me watching her.

'What do you think of Matthew?' she asked at one point. She had got quite near the door but couldn't work out how to turn her face to it and her back to me. I wasn't going to tell her.

'Rather nice,' I said, disjointedly, struggling with the zip. I took all this to mean that she was going to go through everyone to make her questions about Dominic less obvious, so I thought I'd take a short cut. 'But it's Dominic, or Laurie, or whichever, that fascinates me.' I was pleased with this, because she was so caught up with her own subterfuges over the door-handle and Dominic that she didn't notice me playing the same game.

'Yes,' she said, vaguely. 'Me too.'

I was obviously going to have to help her. 'Do my back up, would you?' I turned my back on her and shuffled over. Her cool fingers were as familiar as my own. When she had done, I walked carefully to the side-board, still with my back to her. I heard her move, heard the slight wiggle of her hand on the door knob and gave her plenty of time to turn and stare out of the window. When I looked around, she was staring out of the window.

'Well, if there's nothing else I can do . . .' she said, and walked out.

Christ, you utter bitch! Getting clever too, are we? I kicked the door furiously in my humiliation. Leading me on like that and then walking out . . . 'Hey,' I said, marching in on her. She was squeezing a solitary blackhead in the mirror.

'Ow! You utter bitch! Marching in without knocking like that. What do you want?'

'I want a ring. I thought you might lend me one,' I said, apologetically. 'Have I spoilt your face?'

'No!' She handed me a box. 'Take one of the ones you've had before.'

She looked marvellous in that lacy bra, like a Victorian rape. I thought, no one will ever RAPE Stephanie. I said, 'No one will ever rape you.'

'God! I hope not. What on earth do you mean?' She peered sideways in the mirror to see my face, and I wandered out of range with the box. Anxiously she called, 'Here, which are you taking?'

'How's Peter?' I asked, holding his diamond up to

the light, and squizzing at it against the window. Fancy bringing it here! What cheek.

'Sloppy. Drearily sloppy. If we were still engaged I'd slap his face.' She paused, gloomily contemplating the slapless-ness of being unengaged to Peter. Then she cheered up. 'Maybe I will anyway,' and turned back to the mirror.

I thought the evening might have its better moments after all and took her least posh ring. It was aquamarine and rather dowdy. It suited me. It didn't suit Stephanie. 'Thanks a lot,' I said and drifted out.

◎

While I finished dressing I wondered how Mother was getting on with Marc-Raoul. I wondered if she had proposed yet. She had lent me some of her body lotion and I lavished it about on the parts where I had seen her lavishing it about. It occurred to me that there might be more immediately practical places for me to put it, since Mother's choice of localities seemed curiously inaccessible once I had my dress and stole on, but I couldn't think of anywhere different and decided that it was a general aura of sweetness and perfume that was desirable, rather than a particularised sniff. I thought of Marc-Raoul sniffing, but only drew a blank. Then I tried to think of Daddy sniffing, but it was a long time since I had seen Daddy in his coffin, and that was a blank, too. I wondered where Stephanie put body lotion and decided eventually not to go and ask. I found that I could get quite a good picture of Dominic sniffing. I decided that, generally speaking, my bouquet was good and ambled off to the top of the stairs.

I was fascinated by these stairs. They went down two flights, step by step to the green and white marble floor of the hall. It must have been close on forty or even fifty feet to the bottom. Each step was made of whitened, curved stone and was very shallow and very wide. There could not have been more than five inches between the steps, a fact which ensured either a gracious descent, with one's skirts gathered in one hand like the man said, or a furious scuttling, two at a time. Tonight I picked the former mode. I thought it was a staircase where a lot of things had happened. I was doing some of them on my way down. I needed something other than last year's dress and was feeling ever so slightly put out until I looked up and saw the hooks. Above the centre of the stairwell an enormous glass chandelier swung on a thick chain. I did not doubt that it was real, nor that it had once held candles. The hooks were fastened into the wall on one side and the base of the stair rail on the other. They were of fantastic size. I stopped on the stairs and gazed at them in awe. I saw the little housemaids in their tiny caps leaning out over the rail and picking at the wax on the glass, the vast construction of iron and wire anchored to the hook swung close to the stairs for cleaning. I imagined them looking down forty feet to the marble below and dropping little gleaming kisses of warm water and soap or pellets of wax through the silent morning house. Giggling they disputed the titillating pleasure of releasing the chain so that the tons of glass would swing back, pendulum-like to the wall, return whispering there in the air and then slowly, slowly come to the centre point, weighted, pregnant with death should one drop shiver and a splinter fall on anyone below . . . I thought what a fantastic death it had been for the underfootman speared in the throat by the thin icicle of glass from forty feet above. He had been looking up, and suddenly the blood was very thin and slow about his white shirt and puddling on the polished marble. A cold death, glass and polished marble. I shivered in the high gloom and decided to scuttle instead, but one step at a time. The portraits of horses long fed to the hounds loomed out over my head. Prince, Moray, Bassempourt, Campanilia with foal, Redress and Akond . . . *And when riding abroad does he gallop or walk, or TROT,/ The akond of Swat?* I chanted softly on the first landing. I gathered my skirts, tossed my mane, pawed a fraction at the polished floor, and, about to burst into a full gallop on the straight past the bedroom doors, elbows jabbing my ribs, I halted frozen like Lot's wife. In that most ridiculous of postures, one foot off the ground, head down, elbows out, I looked straight through the door Maria had left open as she came out. She glanced at me curiously and swept by. Her teeth showed, but she was far from smiling. I hardly noticed her. In the room the French woman was reaching out her hand to take a glass. A half empty whiskey bottle stood open on the lace runner beside a hair brush and a trail of black ribbon. John Jameson it said. She was wearing a white robe. It was half open, the belt dangling to the floor. Under it she had black lace briefs on and nothing else at all. (I read in a book in the library how in Siberia they have found a mammoth with a buttercup in its stomach, encapsulated in permanent ice.)

▣

It is a hundred years ago that I saw her breasts pointing out under the white robe. It is nine thousand years since Eve stood in the Garden holding the Apple. I held it in my hands, in my womb, caressing it, squeezing it. Enough to hold it. Time enough to taste. It is nine thousand years since I saw her breasts pointing out under the robe.

◙

The door slammed.

◙

'Helen, Helen, Are you all right?'

Go away, over there, the winds of Eden are blowing over my lumbars.

'Helen! Helen?'

Incarnate I! Only hooks and eyes holding on the cap and bells. Wear them tight about, wear them inside out.

'What's wrong?'

Are you talking to me? YOU to me? Hold it a second now while I whip out my sword and peel back the Durex scabbard. FANTASTIC REDUCTIONS! GOSSAMER 3 doz. £1.15. The night we went to Calary by way of Shanidar. Are you talking to me?

'Helen, for God's sake, come here.'

Ponderously I turned my wide head to look at her. 'Harriet, I think I would like to sit down,' I said primly.

◙

The dead under-footman, the Akond of Swat and I sat on his bed. He had been shaving and still had his glasses on. I was perplexed, not having seen them before. He poured Communion wine and vinegar out of a crystal. We drank it, the vinegar burning our throats, and we looked a little apologetically at each other for we should not have spluttered like that in company. The cover on his bed was made of coarse tweed, Heaven's colour, the Blue. And he said, Death.

'What?' I asked, minding my manners.

I had forgotten that he talked in a foreign language and wept a little, hoping that he would not understand if I cried in English. He was made of birch bark that night, all black and white, with a sheen like silk. I held a torch out and was impressed by the sweetness of the flames when he started to burn. Gabriel, Michael, Raphael . . . Gabriel, Michael, Raphael . . . what pain it was to drown.

'I'm sorry,' I said. I couldn't think of anything else. The blind over my eyes was drawn up, and I looked curiously at the roof of the bed. It was a four-poster. It would be. Harriet's hands were very warm, rubbing my wrists. I asked, 'Are you chafing my wrists?'

'I imagine so.'

'Like in the books?'

'Yes. Just like that. Lie still. You'll fall over if you sit up.'

I fingered the bed cover. It was made of blue tweed. 'Is Dominic in here?'

'Yes,' he said, out of sight. I turned my lacquered hair rasping privately on the bed. There he was.

'I'm sorry,' I said again. 'I think I am in your bedroom.'

'You are. Harry, do put that brandy down, she's had plenty. Helen, would you like a cup of tea?'

'Not quite immediately,' I said, reflecting.

'But by the time it comes?'

'Probably by then I would like it very much indeed.' I was distressed when he went out and I lay miserably waiting for him to come back. Harriet talked a little and put his dressing gown over my feet. They seemed a long way off and looked strange swathed in green silk, but I could feel them again. 'For heaven's sake, don't tell Stephanie,' I jabbered, urgently. 'Please. You won't, will you?'

Harriet looked at me queerly. 'Not if it matters,' she replied.

'It does, oh, it does. It matters awfully—' I wasn't quite sure why, but I knew it was vitally important.

'All right then. Laurie, she says we're not to tell Stephanie.'

So he was back. I looked at the door. He carried a tea tray and had a pair of spectacles on the end of his nose.

'Oh? Fair enough.' He put the tray carefully on the little bamboo table by the bed. 'That put Grogan in a fair spin,' he said. He took the glasses off and tossed them on the bed. It was a double bed, and there seemed to be plenty of room on it, but I could feel them bunching up to me just the same.

Harriet poured out a cup of tea. 'Do you take sugar?'

'No,' I said.

'You do now,' Dominic interrupted. 'They always put sugar in my tea when I faint. It's good for something— your circulation, or your liver, I don't know. In police stations.'

I knew what he meant. I had seen lots of police stations on the t.v. I wondered if he often fainted in police stations, but it seemed rather a personal question so I did not ask. Harriet put two spoonfuls of sugar in the tea and stirred it briskly. I took it. It was revolting. It had the sweet disappointment of Communion wine before breakfast.

'I have a terrible yearning to pull your beads,' Dominic said suddenly, watching me get better as the tea level sank.

I cried out in alarm, 'Please don't—they come off. Look—' I indicated one of the bald patches. 'I did that at the Ripley-Reeves' last year between the tango and the can-can.' Then I added for clarity's sake, 'They were consecutive.'

'Dear me,' he said mildly. 'Who on earth are the Ripley-Raceys to cause such a frenzy of demolition?'

'Ripley-Reeves. She breeds Sealyhams and he breeds donkeys for export to England. They have a daughter who works for the Anti-vivisectionists.'

'My God. And does she breed anything?'

'Well, Stephanie says . . . ' I hesitated, and he grinned.

'What does Steph say?'

'She says she has an illegitimate daughter in Liverpool who is married to a man from County Offaly who runs a knackers yard.' I looked at him doubtfully.

He hooted with derision. 'She may well be right! Would she be old enough?'

'Yes,' I said, not seeing the trap but only his face changing shape because he was laughing. 'The Ripley-R's are seventy odd, the daughter must be nearly forty, and so . . . '

'—If they all started young enough, it is quite on the cards that Steph's revoltingly catty story is quite true. I hope it is. I must ask her all about it, and for an introduction to the Ripsy-R's. May I have some of your tea?'

Like a hostess I dispensed it, lying on his bed. Harriet had some out of the tooth mug, like a midnight feast at school; Dominic drank out of the milk jug. They did not seem put out by the lack of crockery, though I was slightly. I felt all right now, provided I kept my mind on them and put aside the possibility of being sick. Harriet was looking miserable. I thought I had outstayed my dramatic value. 'I must go now,' I said politely, and began to wriggle about on the blue tweed, preparatory to getting up. He was standing by the chest of drawers, doing up his cuff-links. Dimly I remembered Daddy doing that, me standing as high as the buttons on his braces, while he struggled with the starched double cuffs. I remembered the smell of bay rum and earth that he wore—he had been a landscape gardener and had died incongrously in one of his bigger fountains entitled The Vision of Amos which had consequently been demolished. Mother had told me that they had planted a *Salix babylonicus* to mark the spot, so Daddy had died in vain. He hated *Salix babylonicus*, having once spent six months in Welwyn Garden City as an apprentice.

'Have you ever been to Welwyn Garden City?' I asked him. I could not imagine him there, having seen it from a train.

'Yes. Beastly place,' he replied absently, burrowing around his Adam's apple with a stud.

'Laurie—when were you in Welwyn?' Harriet asked suddenly. There was a cold ring in her voice that made me look up in surprise. He turned, disorganised, unprepared, his hands still vague about his throat. 'Before or after Verry died?'

'After,' he answered, his hands becoming purposeful again, his face blank.

'Why did you go?'

'I had some of his things to give back. Books—records—an electric drill—'

'You didn't tell me.'

'NO.'

'I wish I had some of his things. I have nothing of his—' She was suddenly, like a child at Christmas, so deeply in need. 'Yes you have.' He moved at her fiercely. Forgotten on the bed I shrank a little. 'You have, you have, oh, stupid—' He was angry, menacing her across the room, pity become violent in his mouth. I was afraid and would have been anywhere but there.

'Laura?'

'Of course Laura. Oh, stupid.'

She began to cry. I moved at her, gestureless, defence-less. 'Don't . . . ' I said.

'Don't,' he shouted. She stopped. He sat on the bed by her, across the great blue from me. 'Do my collar up, sweet, if you can keep your hands still enough.' When she had done, her face puckered and ugly, he turned to me. 'We were doing so well,' he said. 'You'd never have known, would you, Helen?'

'No. I don't know.' And then because it was necessary and no longer impertinent I asked, 'Who is Laura?'

'Our baby,' Harriet told me. 'Verry's and mine.'

I looked at her left hand. It was naked.

'We weren't married or anything. They all told me I'd be sorry.' She watched him get up and finish dressing. After he had his coat on she said, 'I called the baby after Laurie. Everyone else thought that because we weren't married it didn't matter, you know?'

I could imagine. It's not as if they were married or anything . . . it's not as if she were a widow . . . after

83

all, it's only a very ORDINARY mistake . . . once she's had it adopted and it's all over . . . I heard them all say. I had heard it said at cocktail parties, at tennis parties, behind the palm trees—a very ordinary mistake.

'I wanted to call her Katherine, but Harriet wouldn't have it. I thought what fun I would have with the saucy bits in the 'Shrew' every time she piddled on my trousers.' A very watery grin drifted across the bed.

'That's what god-fathers are for,' Harriet said.

In response he started filling his pockets, looking, I thought, as relieved as any normal male who has got a grin out of two weeping and/or fainting women in his bedroom.

'Gosh!' I said, remembering.

'What?'

'Gosh. Are you all right? I mean, this afternoon—that horse . . . ?'

He laughed at me then, very suave in his dinner jacket. He was incredibly beautiful. 'Oh, yes; I'm all right.'

Harriet stood up and, using his comb, re-did her hair. Mine was still as rigid as the Stars and Stripes in an Alaskan freeze-up, so I ignored it.

'Car keys. Cigarettes-and-lighter. Pen. Hanky . . .' He patted his hips. 'Diary, glasses, more cigarettes, money. More cigarettes . . .' He came close to where I lay, picking up two little chemist's boxes from the bamboo table. I had been noticing them on and off for some time. 'One lot of pills in case one thing happens, and another lot in case another thing happens. That's the lot. Ready?'

'Right,' she said. 'You need a handbag.'

'Go to hell, mate.'

As they walked down the stairs arm in arm in front of me, the vast distance between Helen and Dominic drew out again, almost to infinity. Almost.

◨

Letter xlvi

It is that time of evening now when foxes come out over the larch needles and under the briars in the spinney. The rabbits turn their bursting eyes and ears gratefully into the young dew; saving the owls, the badger, their sons, they will live through the cool night and die of myxie in the morning. On such a night as this Picasso painted the Absinthe Drinker and I made promises to you.

Looking out of my window. No, the curtains are not closed, no matter what you say, I will have my small disobediences, hugging the shriven threads of old comforts close whilst I commit this ultimate obedience to love and offer you my tale. Nay, press you to take it, read it, love me more, and finally, when night comes, lest night come, to take my head between your hands and laying my lips upon your breast to let me weep, and comfort me. O, please comfort me. Comfort me tonight. Love is only labour turned about, and wonder merely question time in Eden.

Looking out of my unprivate window, as far as the distance goes I can see the lights that line the streets. How anxiously they keep steady, in case one little emotion should go stealthily by, unremarked in shadow. Below me one casts up light, searching out my fingers on the Remington taken from the Municipal Library. It fights the light on my table, winning space for its own reflection on the shiny keys, so that not a word, a syllable, a letter shall be palmed away under my fingers. There is Helen, that loves (sic.) Aileen writing yet another love-letter to prop against the Nescafé jar for her breakfast in the morning. So far she has received forty-three letters and two coloured postcards of French Impressionists (viz.) in this way, not counting Christmas, Easter and her birthdays.

But what Big Brother municipal light does not know yet, because I have not yet written it down, is what is going on these forthcoming pages. See below. And it is a different love-letter from the other forty-three and does not say anywhere, except implicitly in the Foreword and here and there in the present tense scenes, I LOVE YOU. And I shall take great care to write some of the more personal paragraphs on my day off, or on Sunday mornings. Big Brother municipal light, I will see you in hell.

I must confess to a certain sense of cosiness in our gathering here in my white-distempered room together. Aileen, Helen, and young Helen, who I used to be when there was Lyn. It is an easy company to find oneself in. And since, as Wordsworth so endearingly put it, the child is father to the man, you must on other evenings have had glimpses of us. But not many of young Helen. This is our first evening with young Helen, who, like Rabbit, had Friends and Relations. Once . . .

Upon reflection I find Wordsworth a little BIOLOGICAL, dear, also sexually inapplicable. And the grammar is obscure. Don't forget to put the rubbish out, the bin men come tomorrow.

Helen

I thought he looked wonderful. His tie was undoing itself, and his jacket was in Himalayan wrinkles about his back. I thought he might be the person to help me. 'Matthew,' I said, 'I want help.'

'Ah, the female condition. Speak on, and I will sort it all out for you, puzzled Little Helen Wykham.'

I knew he wasn't actually being patronising. He would sort it out; I was only five foot four, and I was very puzzled. I sat forward in my white iron chair, my feet among the miniature begonias. We were 'sitting-out', or mutely consenting not to dance with each other again having just knocked over two couples and a small tub of floodlit geraniums and had found a walled-in Italian garden with a formal pool in pale granite. There were chairs and tables littered suggestively about the brink and candles in jam jars flickered among the flowers and dwarf conifers. There were even some night-lights floating in saucers on the water, but most of these had fizzed out because people had disturbed the water to make them dance in the waves, and spray had sodden the wicks. They had been pretty. I had my feet in the begonias because 1 was afraid of falling in. In the centre of the pool a young man was playing *The Death of Jimmy Brown* on a mouthorgan. He was dressed in underpants, socks, suspenders, an elaborately laced shirt front and a paper hat.

Matthew had been studying him gloomily for some time. Now he said, 'I wonder how he got the rest of his shirt off, from under that.' He leaned forward curiously, his eyes screwed up. 'And where it is. It's the sort of thing Dominic would know. Where IS Dominic?'

'In the potting shed with Stephanie.'

'Ah. Is he tight?'

'Certainly not,' I said loyally, taking this to be derogatory to my sister's charms.

'Harriet tells me that he possesses a Van Eyck. I suspect it to be the Renaix Angel, which, as you know, was sold for a stupendous sum to an unknown buyer some months ago. It is the smaller part of a broken painting on a wooden panel and was designed for the altar front of a chapel near Renaix. It has been lost for a couple of centuries. Harriet also tells me that he is only lucid about it when somewhat tiddly. Apparently he can then be induced to wax quite descriptive and doesn't stutter. I should like to hear about the Angel; the other part is in the Gallery in Brussels. And I should like to hear Dominic talking without stuttering. Which is why I wondered if he was tight yet.'

'I see,' I said.

'Now, what did you want help with?'

I took a deep breath. 'If you lurch about like that, you will fall in. What I want to know is, what's going on. I mean, what's going on?'

'That's a very violent question for a pool edge. And you are right. Excuse me while I move my chair back.' He lurched tremendously over the granite facing and settled closer to me, crushing a young *Cryptomeria japonica nana* with the left back leg of the little chair.

I looked at it sadly. 'I think you've just killed a young *Cryptomeria*,' I said.

He glanced nervously over his shoulder at the musician in the pool. 'I have?'

I pointed to the little bush.

'Oh, that. Oh dear. How awful. Can we put it in splints or anything? Or give it a drink?' He poured his gin and french on it carefully. 'Feel better, Mary? Now, what do you mean, what's going on?'

I asked carefully, 'Why does Dominic take pills? Where was Anna when Loftus went mad? Why does Dominic flirt with Stephanie when he's in love with Harriet? Why does Anna hate her mother? Why does the French woman hate Dominic? Who and what was Gerald, and where is Dominic going to?'

Matthew looked at me queerly in the rippling light. I had not noticed before how eerie it was the way the light rippled up from the water. It made all the shadows on his face upside down. 'Got it all taped, haven't you?' he said harshly. 'Like a Girl Guide. Observant and so on. If you can ask the right questions, you can supply the answers. I am not sure that I like this conversation. Shall we go and dance?'

'No!' I cried desperately.

'Come, come. I'm not that bad. I may be clumsy, but I keep time—'

'MATTHEW. I'm frightened. I want to know.'

He turned to the pool, leaning on his knees and staring at the water. With his back hunched up around his neck, he resembled a giant toad, omniscient in the mobile light. 'It's unfortunate,' he said gently, 'that Dominic is such an attractive person. If he were not attractive people would not bother to ask awkward questions about him. Have you any cigarettes? Thanks.'

'Because you think the questions are awkward it means that there is something going on,' I said logically.

'There are two distinct things going on. You have some of your questions in the wrong order. And Dominic is not in love with Harriet. She is in love with him. He sold his soul a year ago, having never loved anyone in his life, to a schoolgirl no one had ever heard of, and that is why he has that funny shut up look. Something happened. One does not know what. One doesn't ask. Gerald was his father, and Maria's lover at some point in their respective youths, and Dominic suffers much violence at his family's hands because he is so like him. Dominic would have it as merely a stamp of the flesh, but I think that may be an underestimation. But it is true that the SanFés generally seem to have failed to distinguish between them, which must have its irritating side. In the end Maria married her first cousin, Anna's father, which is why she never had to change her name, though I doubt very much if she would have, anyway— she finds that being a SanFé gives her scope. So does Dominic, come to that. Gerald then fell in love with, as opposed to sleeping with, Dominic's mother, whom he married, much to Maria's chagrin. As to Anna, she hates Maria because she always has; what makes a daughter hate a widowed mother is something I will not try to understand, and particularly at the moment for being bankrupt again and exposing this to Dominic.'

'Whom she wants to marry her off to, for the price of a collection of Lalique glass,' I added for him.

'And *for the touch of a vanished hand, And the sound of a voice that is still.* Yes. Who told you that?'

'Anna. In a way. And Stephanie, more directly. Well?'

He turned from the water and looked at me. I pressed my hands down into my skirts. He picked one of them up and looked at the ring. 'Pretty. Do we have to talk like this when the nightingales are singing?'

'They aren't.'

'Prosaic Helen Wykham. They could easily be.'

'But they're not,' I insisted. 'And you haven't told me what I want to know yet.'

'Why do you think I should tell you Dominic's secrets? Have you no mercy? Can you not love him a little, with generosity? Well?'

'Tell me where Anna was when Loftus bolted.'

'Oh, Helen, Helen, Helen. Where do you think Anna was?'

'I think she was behind Loftus,' I said slowly. The words fell very distinctly about the pool. I was conscious of pronouncing them carefully.

'Precisely.'

'Is Anna trying to murder Dominic?' I asked finally.

'Goodness me, no. Are you drunk? Even a little drunk? No, no, no, Anna would never do a thing like that.'

'But she would be very relieved if he met with an accident?'

'Of course she would be. Wouldn't you be, if you were faced with the prospect of being lain on by someone you didn't love for the rest of your natural? Or worse, being ignored while he heaved about in a fever of desire for someone else, crying in his sleep, and in his drink, and drinking so that he CAN cry when it's cold between the sheets? . . . Think, girl, think. Imagine it.'

'But Dominic would never marry anyone against her will!'

'Well. There is a tradition that they marry their cousins. It's optional, but they tend to comply. See it from Anna's point of view. Dominic has a vast inheritance to pass on; not this rabbit hutch in the bogs, the goodies on the other side, I mean. Maria has no male heir nearer than Dominic. Anna is—' he paused and looked at me. I was thinking of Mother's lecture in the kitchen. I did not respond to his hint. 'Anna is of marriageable age.

91

Dominic is frustrated and unhappy. Maria is obsessed with Dominic's likeness to Gerald. Dominic ought to breed heirs . . . it's a claustrophobic picture. No wonder Anna has her fears.'

I thought of the goodies in England. I thought of the sweaty sheets, the duty, the effort, and the cold narrow back in winter, of tears. 'It's revolting,' I said plaintively. 'It makes me feel sick.'

'Dominic makes Anna feel sick,' he replied with unwonted roughness, 'so don't ask awkward questions again. Things like this are sickening. I feel sick quite a lot of the time.'

'You put it in such revolting terms,' I complained.

'Hell, you don't think they'd get so frantic if it was just a question of going to the State opening of Parliament looking contented, do you? They'd have to breed. Sons. And go on doing it. Hell . . .'

'Shut up Matthew.'

'Well, you asked.'

I squirmed into myself, the picture wheeling about in my head. O, revolting, revolting. Revolting because it was close, and had to do with me, and things I almost knew about, and knew were revolting. Squalid. People I could imagine, having seen most of them naked in bathing costume. 'Get me a drink, Matthew. I do actually feel sick.'

'I'm sorry; truly, poor Helen Wykham, I'm sorry. But you know, you put me in an awful spot. You asked all the questions I didn't want to have to answer, and you wouldn't be put off.' He put out his great arm, and hugged me like I had always imagined a brother or a father might do. I cried a little into his coat and snivelled into my hanky. But I had a lot more questions to ask.

He said, 'And do you know, I really think you are a little drunk.'

'Yes,' I said humbly, 'I am.' There would be lots of opportunities to ask him the rest. 'And the rest?' I asked, to see.

'The rest is infinitely pitiable, and I am not going to give away another man's pitiful secrets. Come, Helen Wykham, or people will be making secrets about us.' As we left the Italian garden, he said, 'I never knew there were so many verses to *Jimmy Brown*.' The young man was still in the pool.

◻

I left Matthew trying to reach the bar, which seemed to be in a state of siege owing to a rumour that vodka was there for the discerning or for readers of James Bond, into whose world I felt myself to be gaining entry. I wandered off across the crazy paving, for I had another problem which I could not discuss with Matthew. If I got to the yew hedge without being stopped, I would think about it. No one in the herbaceous border to stop me or lurking under the moss to pop up, arrest, terrify. The night was lighter than night should be; perverse glows lit up the cracks between the stones. Water dripped from an over-full gardener's butt. The yew hedge was dark and close with old, acid smells, defeating purpose, recalling instincts no longer given recognition. There was no one in the garden. I might have been my own ghost, trailing my skirts across the stones with the light sound of fever. I was my own ghost. There was not anyone in the garden. I stretched out my hand to the first of the yew. What should have been stringent as pine was silky to the finger tips. I caressed its blackness in the disappointing dark. There had been a moment of transition. My body to spite me, had made it easy; obvious. I could not ignore the obvious. One moment my child's plump shape had bent across the landing, not pretending to be a horse, but more infantile, more undilute than that. Being a horse. In the next moment, a robust woman was looking with lust on another woman's exposed nipples. How to endure it?

Palely as ghost of a ghost the white front of shirt amidst the black, denser than the night. Pale lilies premature, suffer in the hot summer. Francis. Alone, too. 'Do people ever get what they want?' I asked him.

'The Holy Saints and martyrs did,' he said, certainly.

'But people—like me and you?'

Stiffly in the moonshine he replied, 'I hope not.' We sat side by side on a wooden seat recessed into the yew hedge. The garden was sweet around us, damascened with starlight. The shadows of night light are not urgent. It seemed a very simple thing, sitting in the night light with a young man, in a private garden. A very old and very simple thing to do. Maybe, I thought, one day, maybe . . .

'I would rather have peace than what I want,' Francis said thickly. 'I want to be a priest. But it seems a bit difficult—just now. Don't tell.'

Alien, alien thought. Too alien; too rare. For once I had no word. No thought. No glittering drop of comfort. Francis became something other in the flesh. Shocked I looked at him, but he did not see my pain. He had drawn his feet up on the slatted seat and was hugging his knees and some private horror of his own. Topsy found us there, side by side in the dark hedge, like a couple conceived by Tennyson, smiled brightly and was brief with us. We

94

went with her to dance again, guilty, as if we had been caught in some minor infidelity to her, or our hostess.

◙

'Dominic—I want to talk to you,' Matthew said firmly.

'Oh yeah? Pass that bottle, Harry my love.'

'About Van Eyck.'

'Van Eyck?'

'Van Eyck,' Matthew repeated.

Dominic looked around vaguely. 'He's not here tonight,' he said apologetically, after a pause. 'But there are lots of others here. Would one of them do?'

Matthew looked forlornly at me. 'Too late, much too late,' he murmured. Dominic was certainly far from sober. He seemed to have retreated on to a personal inebriated roundabout, which rotated past Stephanie's bust, the wine bottle, the band, and back to Stephanie. He could not be deflected from any of these, nor would he permit the sequence to be interrupted.

'That bottle,' he was saying. 'Why should it be green? It doesn't have green wine in it. It is pale yellow. Why therefore should it not be in a pale yellow bottle? Or is the wine yellow—is it not green?' He picked up his glass and peered at it. Then, carrying it carefully he weaved away down the line of fairy lights suspended from the guttering. Under a green one he stopped. Considering every move he held the glass up to the little pointed bulb. His arms were enormously long. The amber links caught the light so that the graven lilies became distinct and hard as his wrist moved. 'Look,' he said with complete satisfaction, 'it IS green!' He drank it gleefully. 'Green inside,' he murmured. He unbuttoned his shirt and looked inquisitively at his stomach.

'Laurie, for heaven's sake! Do your shirt up.'

'Harry, my love, the night breezes are wafting down my tummy, and very soothing they are. I will not do my shirt up.' He flopped on to the ground, crosslegged and faced the heavy bulk of the mountain in the starry sky. 'Blow, blow,' he chanted to the stirring in the formal shapes of ornamental trees, his eyes half shut, his face lifted to the sky. The band stopped playing. He listened to the accompanying noise, adjustment to the withdrawal of rhythm; the low sound of too many people turgid with their own enjoyment.

I watched him anxiously. It was the stuff of life to me to be stirred by him now. I had to be. His beauty, softened but not yet blurred by the drink, tugged at me a little, but too little. Tugging at the wrong part of me. Not so Stephanie. Her little lips were glistening in the fairy lights. I envied her as I had never envied her before.

Topsy and Francis came back from the floor, he still morose with his thoughts, she unaware and content, holding his hand pretending that he was holding hers.

'The band have gone for their supper,' she announced to make an entry. Obediently we all turned and looked at them. Obediently we noted the clasped hands. Francis flushed under Dominic's glance and disengaged himself. There was one of those awful hushes among the party that occur for no reason. Topsy swept around, bustling with the bottle. Her dress caught a glass and it shattered on the stone of the patio where we were gathered. The fragments leaped and vanished under feet and skirts as the horde of dancers swept past us, flowing over the glass splinters and Dominic, unperturbed and incurious.

'Laurie, are you sober?' Bill said suddenly, stepping out of the shadow where he had been leaning over Harriet's chair, his hands in her hair. 'Harriet, is he sober?'

'I wouldn't think so, but he's probably soberer than he looks. Laurie?'

Dominic rubbed his hands furiously together. 'Now, what's all this about Van Eyck?' he said to Matthew. Bill yelled. Dominic's eyebrows began twitching, and he got up from the floor. 'I'm as drunk as a lord, as sober as a judge, as right as a Ribstone Pippin,' he announced. 'Helen, dear child, alas I cannot both play the Charleston and dance it. Therefore we won't play it. But it is on request, and I demand the privilege for later. Stephanie, if I find you buggering about with anyone else I'll thump you. I'll send over a great plate of cherries and ice cream to keep you quiet. O.K.?'

'Give it a rest, do.' Stephanie's slanted eyes were greedy on him. I blushed furiously at being addressed. Topsy stared at me crossly.

'If you ever want to shut her up, Helen,' he went on, fumbling in his pocket, 'give her cherries and ice cream. Where the hell did I put my glasses?'

'Left hip,' I said, unconsciously.

'Ah. Thanks.' He put them on his nose, his arm round my sister. Her eyes were like saws between her lashes. Peering down her cleavage he said, 'Gracious, I must wear them more often. Now where's this chap James or Fred, or whatever?'

He kissed Stephanie rapturously and suddenly on her open, angry mouth, pulled Bill by the sleeve, whispered something to Harriet and vanished through the french doors in the direction of the bandstand.

97

'What on earth,—?' I asked.

'How the fucking hell—?' Stephanie hissed.

Harriet giggled and I had an urge to hit her. They were all looking at me, and I could feel the tumescent heat of shame crowding about me and within me because I knew where his glasses were. But I had nothing to be ashamed about except being noticed—being obvious. How blithe Topsy would have been in my place; how silky my sister; WHY CAN'T I BE LIKE THAT?

'—and hear them.'

'What?'

'Come in and hear them. Dominic and Bill, and a couple of others.'

There was a tradition that when the band went to supper one of the amateur groups, of which there were many, would take over, until the band returned. Usually they were people we knew, and we were impressed by their skill, envious of their talent, desirous to be seen dancing with them for half-an-hour or so afterwards. I followed Matthew, wondering how Dominic and Bill, who were after all strangers, had acquired the privilege.

You would have had to be tone-deaf to miss it.

They were generous with him, or maybe it was etiquette; leaving him plenty of solo time, hunched over the piano. He returned the compliment to Bill who had the sax but not to James on the drums, or the other Bill with the trumpet. He was too professional for that. They were not in the same class.

Nor even was Bill.

The band pianist returned to the room with a sandwich in his hand. He was followed by the leader and then the other two. The dancers stopped rotating, and slunk, abashed, hand in hand to the walls.

You would have had to be deaf to miss it.

You would have had to be blind not to see it.

It stopped being fun; I remember when the other three joined in with him, how I found myself frowning and noticed others caught the same way. The band leader was very clever. People drifted away chatting, the young men voluble and excited, the girls quietened, maybe depressed a little. He got them all back on form by inciting them to sing silly popular songs, as far from blues as music could go. Dominic himself disappeared. I heard Bill say to someone that he had been to the South and had heard and played real jazz there. They had played together in Oxford before Laurence went to America. No, he didn't know what he had done there; no one did. He wouldn't talk. Yes, yes he was a musician, he had once been professional; no, not jazz—I found my eyes locked in Matthew's.

'We shall can-can together, so you will have no breath left to ask questions with,' he announced. We did. No one near us had any breath left either. Matthew doing the can-can had much the same mesmerising effect on his neighbours as if Goliath had done a minuette to encourage the Philistines.

I was desperately glad I was a bit drunk and would have been quite happy to have been more so. I became more so quite quickly; the can-can had given me an outrageous thirst, and I was feeling hunted by an emotion which I recognised with horror, as something akin to pity. It was his face, when he had turned from the piano, to disappear alone into the garden . . . blessed garden, planted for solace, affording so much comfort that night. Stephanie became frosty and cold-eyed in his absence, claiming Matthew as a rearguard defence. He was soft on her. People were always soft on Stephanie, even when she was like sharp ice. I knew she was questing after Dominic because her eyes were straying; she usually kept them fixed and half closed on her partner, although partner does not seem quite the right word to describe the second of a pair of which she was one. Accomplice has a more evocative accuracy. Bill was making the most of Dominic's absence, as he had threatened to do, his nose pressed lasciviously against Harriet's ear in the dimming lights. We had reached that stage of the evening when the bulbs are mysteriously extinguished one after the other. Topsy had removed Francis to be admired by some of our acquaintances whose company I was content to be without. I felt sorry for him, but he seemed quite happy when I looked. I realised with a start that he was imitating Dominic. I shuffled behind a non-functioning Connemara marble gas standard with a large frilly shade and watched him. He had all Dominic's tricks off, but they seemed affected in him, though Topsy and the others didn't appear to be disturbed by this. I saw him light a cigarette, holding the match between his first and second fingers, the flare away from his hands, and chortled vindictively to myself. I had done this too; I knew all about this; the selection of tiny details that make the fantasy suddenly valid. I knew, too, what was due to happen and wondered how he would take it. I watched the way he stood, used his hands as he talked, shifted his shirt sleeves uneasily, as if they were a trifle short, although they were long enough. It was not Francis but Dominic who had the long arms. Anna, punctiliously foxtrotting with Peter, jogged past, her shoulders lifted uncomfortably high to accord with his height. She was truly tiny. Her eyes caught Francis, and he turned his back on her, suddenly convincingly rude. I hugged my arms in pleasure. I was quite private tucked in here behind my lamp standard. I could watch, giggle, dissect, analyse all alone in the shadow; I would note, remember and re-enact those bits that caught my fancy later, in the isolation of my friendly, private life. I took my pleasure where I could get it in those days, like a camel humping through a desert. It did not bother me to be alone and without a partner. It was better that way, so long as no one saw. That was why I was hiding behind the lamp. Sometimes, if there was no hiding place, I would go and read in the lavatories. I had a large library of paperbacks I had begun on lavatories in other people's houses, and had taken away to finish. I wrote the date and circumstances in the fly-leaf, which must have vexed anyone who subsequently borrowed them from me. It give me a masochistic thrill to write 'McCormick's dance, Fitzwilliam Sq. Penultimate dance' below the title. So now I huddled in under the beige tassels and watched and waited. It struck me that Anna and Peter danced exquisitely together, both with the same absorbed interest in getting the steps right. I wondered if Bill knew about Harriet's baby, or if he minded. I wondered what it was like to dance so close to someone who had had someone else's baby. I wondered why she had kept it; why she had not married the man with the funny name before he died. Maybe she hadn't known, then. I wondered what inaccurate information Stephanie was passing on to Matthew, and where it would ultimately come to rest. I wondered what the bloody hell I was doing behind a defunct lamp standard, wondering. Morose and discontent with my lot, I emerged to find myself face to face with Dominic.

'Good evening,' he remarked.

Ooh, he was smooth. 'Grrr,' I said, like Uncle Nick's dachshund.

To my mortification he flung his head back, and exposing his thin throat and genuine pearl stud to my astonished eyes, he howled like eight couple of hounds in full cry.

'Shut up,' I hissed, as heads turned, 'Oh, do shut up!'

He delivered himself of a very passable imitation of the *Gone Away* on the horn, shot out his arms and away we went like two bats out of hell, up and down and round and round till my feet got tangled and my eyes went black and we fetched up back under the Connemara lamp. I was aware of the superficiality of Francis' imitation. 'Drink, drink, drink, till your sister has finished telling tales to your pal Matthew.'

'How do you know she is telling tales?' I demanded haughtily.

'Everyone tells tales to Matthew. It's his job to make them. Didn't you know?'

I thought, in view of my recent experience with Matthew, that this line should be dropped. In any case, I was dizzy. Also, I burned all over. I felt like a junkie deprived of dope. I yearned all over where his body had touched mine. My hands, my back, anywhere where I had felt him, I was a yawning nothing. A Henry Moore, with gaps to tell where the losses were. So this is it. THIS IS IT. I FEEL IT. I CAN FEEL IT. O, Dominic, Dominic, I CAN FEEL IT. I said, 'O God, thank you,' and started for the bar.

'Jesu! I didn't realise you were that thirsty.'

I could feel him following. You know? Actually feel it. Like on the beach when I had known he was a long

102

way off, and then close to, without looking. I could feel the skein of sensation tangling me up in him; I wasn't going to have to miss it all, I knew I wasn't. I knew to a millimetre how close his arm was to my back, how much above my hair his jaw was, I was unstartled when he jostled me in the crowd, hard as iron, as beautiful as an angel; my Iron Angel come back after all. O, God, thank you . . .

Later someone said Dominic was ill. Crouched over my drink (I had not moved from the bar), I knew dismay. He had gone after Stephanie, and I had sat drinking, too moved by my own emotion to care who saw that I was unaccompanied. I had danced once or twice with boys whose mothers I knew, the reasons were obvious, and with Francis. He had the sense not to do a Dominic on me though, and it was a stilted, politic affair. Maybe he thought his big cousin might be checking up on his manners. Maybe I was bloody minded and uncouth. Maybe he was privately elevating the Host with escalator arms like an El Greco painting. I don't know. Neither of us enjoyed it. Nor did Topsy, who was looking more like a Victorian governess than an art student. We parted, relieved that it was over and not to come, and here was this beastly woman perched on the sofa only ten inches from my goosey elbow, saying, 'My dear, that enchanting young man who played the piano, you know (so reminiscent—exactly like the things Willie and I used to hear on the wireless when we were courting you know)—' Christ—Get ON with it . . . WHAT about him?—'—well, I was in the blue spare room, next door to where the furs are, and I just happened to peep through the door beyond—you do have such wonderful wallpapers, dear, and there he was!'

Our hostess said 'Oh.' Considering the build-up and Dominic's looks she may be forgiven. One doesn't actually want to be told about sex in the spare bedroom, but it's reassuring to a hostess to know that it's happening. Discreetly.

'Flat out, my dear, with a BRANDY bottle and no trousers. Well, naturally, I thought, I mean to say—'

'What did you think, dear?'

'Lucetta, don't be come-uppish. I thought exactly what you are thinking I thought. But he was quite alone, and after a while I came to the conclusion that he was not drunk but ill. Now I've told you, and I think you ought to tell someone, or do something.'

The informant sat back, bridling a little, but defiant. I had a momentary liking for her. But it vanished and I was numbed. I felt the dread pity flicker and stir, and nearer to me, somewhere just under the surface, just below the brain, a disappointment that weighted the hollows in my bones. And still I could only think, O God, thank you. I can feel this too. Thank you.

So the hostess went away and told Anna. And Anna shrugged distastefully and told Harriet, and Harriet took a long drink and told Bill, and he disappeared. And I sat like a lump of cold, misformed lead and waited with my gin and tonic.

After an eternally long time it was Dominic who appeared first. They all looked at him, and then they all looked at each other, and except for being a little quiet he betrayed no emotion whatever, but took Stephanie off into a lethargic waltz in the semi-dark, where I could see her white hand caressing the side of his neck. Once again I found myself looking at Matthew.

'Well?' he said.

'Well?'

'That is the other thing that is going on.' And once again I found it hard to believe him.

'You talk like a tragedian,' I accused him, bending my neck to glare up at him.

'I am. I watch tragedy, but God forbid that I should have to take part in it. I have no stomach for such things.'

I did not understand him, and eyed him distrustfully as Bill came up. 'Where is Harriet?' he asked.

Matthew gestured at a door that had Mesdames pompously stencilled on the inside of a dress box lid.

'Is she all right?'

'My dear man, I can scarcely go in and enquire. I imagine she is.'

Bill looked upset, and shifted about. Eventually he said, 'Look, Matthew, get me a drink of whiskey, will you?'

Matthew looked put upon, but went. Bill turned to me. 'Go in there and tell Harriet that Laurence is O.K.'

I was frightened and did not want to go. I thought of what Matthew had said. I looked for Dominic but could not see him in the dark. I looked at Bill. 'Go on,' he said viciously. I went.

Harriet was standing by the window of the downstairs cloakroom, her feet among the Wellingtons and dog leads, her face turned against someone's tennis-racquet. There were criss-cross marks on the side of her nose. 'Hello,' she said quickly, pretending to be doing something to her zip.

'Bill says Dominic's all right,' I said nervously. Her eyes were like glimpses of barbed wire. 'He's dancing,' I added. 'Dominic, I mean. Bill is waiting for you outside.'

'Thanks,' she said, briefly. 'I'll be along.'

Dismissed I turned to go. Then I turned around. She was burrowing in her bag, her hair flopping in great lanky streams across her squared face. I couldn't see her expression. 'What's the matter with him?' I asked.

'Laurie? Oh, his insides don't work.' She didn't look up, and I did go then.

My voice had sounded strange to my ears, flat, unemotional. It is a tone I know well, now. I smiled at Bill, told him she was coming, ignored Matthew's outstretched hand, and returned to the sweet formal gardens of that place. Beyond the Italian pool where I had sat with Matthew the lawns reached out among the cedars and ginkos, lighter and longer for being unlit and beyond each heap of sprawling shadow under the high trees, further spaces of starry dew trailed away toward the great bulk of mountain that seemed to rise sheer from the garden's boundary. It was an enchanted place, and unpeopled, even by ghosts. My feet found the grass and grew wet and cold. I came to one of the cedars and sat under it, my naked back against the trunk, and thought about vomit. I wanted to think about beautiful things, like pale long hands on counterpanes, or cool linen on hot foreheads, or a flickering pulse in a thin wrist . . . fluttering was really the expression. I thought of Matthew's phrase, 'infinitely pitiable' and rejected it in terror. I thought about diarrhoea. I wanted to run away among the quiet trees, my hands over my mouth, to the heather streams on the slope above. I wanted this new Thing to go away. I picked at the needles under my hands and prayed for it to go away. For Dominic to go away. For the thoughts he engendered to go away. Beds. Beds are disgusting. No one should be asked to rest in a bed. They are foetid stews of exudations. How can I ever sleep again in a bed, which is a place where Dominic vomits and sweats; where unloving husbands turn to the wall and drench their own bellies in their dreams; where Harriet grunts and heaves in the slippery blood and shrieks for a dead man. I moaned and twisted beneath the cedar, fighting the lumps of gin in my stomach and the fury in my head. Curse Matthew for what he told, and how he told it; curse Stephanie for her sly hints on winter evenings when, miraculously, she was at home and wanting to boast . . . With each curse I dug my hands into the soil around the bole of the cedar, flinging earth, rotten granite chips, cedar needles and dog-shit at my pointed evening slipper. I made quite a business of it, to smother that which was too far down even to be thought. O God; this is the very stuff of comedy. I was sick, not a whit theatrically, and forgot Dominic in my misery, scuffing around among the tree roots to cover it over.

Dawn. Out over the sea, a novelty in time. Different from every other dawn as the second from the first. And hideously cold. Feeling very thin I went back across the lawn. They had got to *Good night, Sweetheart, see you in the morning*— as I passed the door. Which was patently ridiculous, as it was already so far morning that despite the extinguished lights they could see each other quite clearly. I went on, beyond the room where the coats were and found a bathroom where guests were not expected. All the same, there was something floating in the lavatory pan, and I peered at it for some time before I recognised what it was. We didn't have contraceptives in Holy Ireland. Or we said we didn't. Certainly I had never encountered a used one in a pink lavatory before.

I couldn't quite bring myself to sit on the seat even after I had flushed the thing round the bend, so I peed most uncomfortably with my bare bottom sticking out into the cold behind me, like a sheep, and then sat on the side of the bath reading an Agatha Christie called *Why Didn't They Ask Evans?* until I heard the National Anthem. As I had finished Chapter I, I didn't replace it beside the bath but stuffed it into my evening bag to add to my collection. I was very experienced and so was apparently just arriving from the dance floor when Stephanie came in to find her coat. I seldom had a partner for the last dance, but I do not think many people were aware of the fact. We were as polite as we always were when we weren't quarrelling, but it took Harriet to say, 'Where on earth were you? Matthew has been galloping up and down the house like a lost sheep dog.'

Stephanie managed to look both supercilious and suspicious at the same time and answered for me. 'Helen leads a life of her own that we wot not of.'

Too bloody right, she didn't wot of it; she only wotted of one thing as was apparent from the handkerchief she was smoothing her eyebrow with, which had L.D.M.S. on one corner and a smear of her own lipstick on another. Also she was wearing a perfume of startling similarity to the after-shave lotion or whatever that I had noticed on L.D.M. bloody S. And I didn't wot of that thing at all, so I cried and said I was drunk and due for a bout of malaria.

◨

The door slammed in the everlasting wind that blows on Calary. I heard him moving about below me. He had failed me. Even his beauty had failed me. He was sick; rotten in the core. He had rejected his talents, taking them down into the dark mines inside himself; burying them deep; he had loved, and it had borne no good fruit. Everything he touched turned black, became fit only for burial. I buried some of my hopes that night, too. Deep down, below his footsteps. My little, weak, contrary hopes, that one day I might be like other girls. I killed that hope, because Dominic had failed me. I thought it was the last night of so many nights that would never come again; that it was the end of so many things, some so happy, some terrible; like the night before a marriage, or the night after a death. I heard the hall clock strike eight, and I was very conscious of the bog around the house and the length of time it had been there, and the succession of steamy, summer mornings like this one, that had meandered over its indifferent reflections. Before I fell asleep, I wept for Lyn as I hadn't wept for more than a year.

◉

Aaa-hh. Don't, aah don't, dear Doreen, whoever your progenitors may have been, don't wake me up like this in your wig-like perm, 70p on Saturdays in Enniskerry. I ached in every limb, shivered in dried sweat, felt my double chin quadruple in the sun, my tongue as gruesome as dry-rot fungi, my eyes clogged and weak. O God. I muttered kindly intentions at Doreen, who looked at me with the loathing the wakeful always have for the smeared sleepy, and felt wounded and hardly done by when she whisked the faded curtain back and let that awful, yellow sun rush at me in my closet of misery.

'Seemed a bit queer bringing tea at this hour, miss, so I done you a Nescaff instead,' she said happily.

Terrified that she might at any moment break into that grotesque tap-dance that the Irish do, when they dress up in kilts and play bagpipes, I shooed her out, by dint of lurching on to my elbow and sneezing. My pyjamas had come undone and my right breast dangled out of the gap between the button holes. It was all hideous and unmanageable. I had dreamed all morning about mad horses and French shutters, and of all unlikely things, a cave man complete with bone, dissecting a history book with a piece of broidery-anglais. It was not propitious, I decided.

The Nescafé was fantastic. Woefully I looked at the bottom of the cup. Gone. O, the grief of it. There were little flowers at the bottom of the cup, hand painted blue and silver roses. Dear goodness, they were pretty enough, but would that they had been covered with that merciful liquid. I was contemplating the shattering inevitability of dressing myself up in my mauve dirndl skirt when I heard the noise next door. The noise came through the wedge of newspaper and sellotape in the blocked-up keyhole and was nothing more weird than Dominic's voice. He had a marvellous voice; it made little nerve ends twitch all over me. But I wasn't thinking about that now. I was thinking that on the other side of the keyhole was Stephanie's bedroom; and that there was an unlikely pleading tone in his voice; and that if I listened very hard I might learn something to my advantage. So I did. I listened so hard that I forgot about my mauve and nearly stopped breathing. What I learned was so astonishing that I nearly spoiled everything by leaping out of bed, thundering around the floorboards and clanking my ear to the keyhole. What he was saying, crossly, and with a lot of stammering, was that Stephanie was a prude. My idea of a prude and my idea of Stephanie did not coincide at any point. It transpired, from what I could hear, that she had sat about half the morning waiting for him to come slinking up to her room, lying in bed, STAYING AWAKE for him! And it was now lunch time; she had finally gone to sleep for about a quarter of an hour, had been roused by a bloody nosey housemaid, was feeling ghastly, and in he marched, drunk, randy, and totally immodest, with everyone awake and broad daylight. And did he think she was a ——ing WHORE or what. Note of finality.

He filled in the blanks for her. She provided more in the same strain. He wanted to know what was wrong with lunch-time anyway? She said it was indecent. That was when he laughed at her and called her a prude. But he was very cross. He slammed the door when he went out and left me hugging myself with a near hysterical delight. I knew what Stephanie was like when she was frustrated, and what she was like after a short night, and the idea of her being assaulted in her bed by Dominic when everyone was drinking pre-luncheon sherry downstairs was too funny to be endured. I thought of her, staying awake, listening for his footsteps, trying not to get her make-up smudged on the sheet, while he sat on the terrace with the whiskey bottle, and the sun rode higher and fiercer over the bog. I had never thought about Stephanie-Rejected before and found it hugely entertaining. I wondered which of her eight nighties she had been wearing while she waited. Then I remembered how ill he had looked at the end of the dance, and how there had been strange, new lines all over his face, and

I shook with a cold fury that she could be so stupid and so selfish as to think that he would go to her bed to be comforted. It occurred to me then that Stephanie, like me, had a passion to be loved. That she ached to perform that other feminine role which is non-erotic and which she had never been allowed to act out, because her handicap was the beauty I envied her. I remembered how often she was snubbed in conversation if she stepped out of the role of lightweight seductress which had been given her to play; how I myself did it; and how Mother had laughed at her one day when she had spoken of her future. I remembered it very clearly. We had been hutched up in the conservatory one wet spring day, Mother leaning over the bench with a watering-can to sprinkle the tall, lacy ferns she grew in there and Stephanie acknowledging in a subdued tone that she thought she might try physiotherapy as a career. Mother had peered out over her sun-glasses, laughed heartily and said, 'Pet, you'd have all your cases back in men's surgical with epididymitis.' Stephanie and I had looked up the long word, and she had been very quiet for a week and soon after had begun staying out all night. I think she would have given every one of those nights for the chance of Dominic coming to her bed for comfort, just as he must have longed for a night without tenderness. I suppose none of us had the right thing to give, nor offered it to the right person. My feeling sorry for Stephanie was a new emotion and a disconcerting one. I had a great desire to stop her from whacking her case and drawers in and out, so I got up and tottered feebly in to her.

'Hello,' I said, spinelessly. She was brushing her hair with curt strokes as if she would have it out. She ignored me. She had been wearing her dark blue nightie, the one she had made herself with white lace off her Confirmation veil on it. 'How are you?' I said.

'Fine.'

'Did you enjoy the dance?'

'Yep.' Brush; brush-brush-brush.

'What's the matter with Dominic?'

'Dunno.' Brush.

'He rides well.'

'Oh?' Brush-BRUSH.

'Nice weather.'

Down went the brush. Kissing noises of lipstick.

'I like this house.'

Kiss-kiss.

It suddenly occurred to me that I had come in to tell Stephanie what to do with one of her men. ME—HER. 'Well, cheerio, then,' I said, and went back to my mauve dirndl. As a conversation it hadn't been much of a success. All I had wanted to do was to say, Look, matey, you give him one night without sympathy and you'll have given him more than comfort and more than sex. And it'll be the best night's work either of you have ever done. But I hadn't. I never would. Anyway, how the hell did I know? But I did. Perhaps I ought to join the C.I.D. as a female tec. This was a serious possibility till I thought of the robbers. I wasn't much of a physical hero. A fact which I proved that very afternoon. I missed lunch and couldn't pluck up the courage to walk in late. In any case the smell made me feel sick. It was meaty and high. I peeped in through the dining room window and there they all were, and my place was conspicuously empty. I knew Stephanie would make an adequate excuse, not so much for me, as for her sister. I was content to let her carry me in these matters. I was busy.

I had been out for a couple of hours before I came to the dolmen. I had been wandering over the surface of the bog, my footsteps insubstantial where the wind screamed in January, my shadow heavy on the sphagnum where only cloud shapes floated under the sky. I had been feeling for Lyn among the black, acid moors. The higher the bog, the deeper the peat beneath my feet, the further away she was from me and the sharper the pain of distance. Every heather root, all the minute, emerald foliage on the squamose pools; each colourless efflores- cence on the brittle juncus grass and the distrait beauty of the silver cotton; all these wild extremes of moorland and bog were natural to me and as much part of my physique as the lungs which breathed the brown damp or the soles of my feet which felt the give and take of tussock and drift. I had been born and raised to the bogs. Wherever I go, however long I may stay and grow to love some other place, only the bogs will ever give me peace. I think it must be so for everyone. I do not mean a positive gift, but rather a negation of interference; an acceptance that is deeper than pleasure, that is only realised when one is in one's native habitat. Any other air that is not sea and moorland air is alien to me. My sleep patterns fail, my breathing becomes tetchy and dry. Not so that I would ever be ill, and sometimes after acclimatisation, so slight that I am scarcely aware of the alteration; but, returning, I am each time aware of deep, physical ease. For every man there must be such a habitat; for some the laden breath of cities must surely have given rise to a physical or chemical protection, or sieve, which in the highlands suffers neglect, disfunction, and so produces all those minimal tensions and dis-easeful dreams which frighten us and break our lives up into tragedy or farce. It was this that was giving me such pain now. My perverse body was craving for the stringent sensation of the chalk lands, like a drunk or an addict.

Where Lyn lived, high above the Avon, the soil was thin enough to pick off with the finger nail. Strange sweet smells, strange bright lights, harsh brilliance of the white dust on the wheat and on the short turf grass, these alien experiences were all the sensuous life I had of her. Yet it was vivid enough, and I was lusting for it. Where I saw gorse I needed juniper; where I saw cotton I had visions of harebells; where I trod heather I felt plantain; where I fingered bracken I touched orchids. Each stalk, each stem, each leaf, each sepal gave me pain, as I wandered on the face of the bog.

The dolmen was built in a little hollow, just above a stream, on the slope of the hill. I wandered into the hollow following a sheep track and sat with my back to one of the big stones where the sheep had scratched and left wisps of greasy wool in the weathered cracks of the granite. I was listening for the sound of the larks that quiver over the downs in June when I saw someone coming towards the dolmen down the valley. I slithered on my bottom around the vast upright, because I was unwilling to be seen and have my melancholia dispersed in fruitless exchanges with some shepherd's wife or rabbit-hunting urchin. Consequently I did not see Anna until she appeared inside the dolmen, looming like a hugh symbol of herself beside the crack between the stones where I was sitting. I kept very still, thinking she would look about and go, but to my dismay she sat down, back to back with me on the other side of the same stone. The dolmen was composed of four upright stones of enormous bulk with a great slab balanced as a roof across the top.

The roof stone was not even, being several feet thick at the front edge and diminishing to a matter of inches at the back where I was sitting, so that it gave a severe backward slope to the upper, outside surface, although it was nearly horizontal inside. Anna was sitting on the ground inside, facing the biggest gap between the stones which served as an entrance. She could see anyone coming down the valley and because of the siting of the dolmen on the slope she could also have seen anyone for half a mile around, unless they had been deliberately hiding from her as I had been. I was curious as to what she might be doing, alone there. After all, she had eight guests to entertain, and she was usually punctiliously polite. It occurred to me that they might be going to have a picnic tea or something and that I would have to emerge, shamefacedly from my seclusion as they milled about making fires and flirting in the sun. I was about to get up and announce my presence in order to forestall this eventuality when I heard a curious scraping sound from the other side of the stone. I peered through the crack. Anna was holding a garden trowel and appeared to be digging up the inside of the floor. I wondered if she were an amateur archaeologist, looking for bones or gold or whatever they do look for in dolmens. I became intensely curious and a little patronising about other people's hobbies as the scratching and scraping went on, and I sat in the sun with my back to the warm stone, listening for the merry little cries of a House-party Having a Picnic. But the sound Anna was making was not merry. It was a soft little noise I had only heard once before, coming from behind the sea wall at Bulloch Harbour one moonlit night. I had peered around thinking to see a seabird or even a seal stranded on the sloping bulwark, but there had been semi-naked humans writhing in the shadows and I had crept guiltily away. I strained my neck to get a better view of what she was doing. She straightened up at almost the same second blocking my view so that I was none the wiser. Moving away, she pulled what seemed to be fuse wire from her pocket and spent some time fiddling with that. When she emerged I was sufficiently embarrassed and disturbed to dodge around the stones, keeping well out of her sight. I knew how to move quietly; it is one of the first things the totally dishonest learn, and we must have been half an hour playing this lurid hide-and-seek around the placid dolmen. She moved stones, she darted in and out, she paused for breath and thought, and all the while made this mounting mewing sound that made me cold in the blaze. She did not ever see me; I knew about shadows, I knew about sound. At last she went, walking quickly away down the valley. She did not look back. She was on the skyline when she met someone else. From his height it must have been Matthew. Motionless I watched her gesture behind her at the stones. He started down the valley towards me. He changed his mind and accompanied her over the brow and out of sight. When I was absolutely certain that they had gone, I emerged out of the shelter of the stone and crept inside. I went tentatively, on hands and knees. I don't know why I was afraid, but it seemed suddenly very cold in the stone womb. I thought of Anna meticulously brushing down her skirt when she first came out; of her little hands brushing hair from her eyes, and how there had been no hair across them. A sheep bleated sadly, a long way off; a single lost Suffolk, no doubt, mourning for the familiar fat watermeadows of its homeland as it struggled with the grasping heather and jerked its little pointed feet from the sucking mires.

It was dull in the dolmen. The soil was pale and powdery. Sheep droppings, two attenuated human copro-lites, a cigarette packet and a rusty bicycle chain cluttered the entrance. I circumnavigated them with caution and hesitated. I was almost exactly where Anna had started her digging. Six inches from my left shoulder was the gap between the two stones that formed that side of the dolmen. The other side wall was made of one much larger slab, and the rear wall by the fourth slab. I sat back on my heels and looked about. It took me a minute or two to spot it. I would not have seen it if I had not been looking, and looking in fear. The boulder was wedged in the crack between the two stones of the left wall. It was well above my head height and just above the average man's. It was held against the roof slab by the wire which passed around it, outside through the gap between the stones, inside through the heather and around the foot of the entrance where I had just crawled, and was now lying directly in front of me, obscured by an old paper-back, some scuffed earth and sheep wool. It was secured finally to a peg on my right. I could see that the earth was disturbed, and carefully sprinkled back, so that no footmarks or trodden places would draw the eye down on entering. The boulder was not big; it would not kill. It might break a limb or cause concussion. There was no room to avoid it. Whoever trod on the wire, jerked up the poised peg and released the boulder would certainly be hurt. Equally certainly they would not be killed. I must have taken ten minutes getting my right knee and two hands out over the section of the wire I had already crossed. I was shaking in every limb. Sweat poured into my eyes and down my ribs, and my hands were past praying for. I sat in the sunlight and I shook and I shook. When I was able to stand up I didn't know what to do, so I looked about till I found the bicycle chain. To reach it I would have had to lean against the stone around which the wire passed. I couldn't possibly have released the peg and disturbed the boulder; the stones had been leant on for four thousand years and looked pretty steady. And even if I had, I was well out of range. But I couldn't do it. I just shook instead. I found a small piece of rotten granite in the bracken and threw it at the wire, but I missed it by several feet. I couldn't find another. I shook some more. I inspected the outside section of the wire. She had rubbed wool and soil over it so it would not catch the eye. I tugged at it, but I was tugging against the boulder and only wedging it harder, not releasing it. I heaved at it from below and a thin trickle of blood sprang up on my palm. I shook again and cried a bit. I lay on my tummy in the entrance and flailed hysterically at the wire with a piece of heather, but it wasn't strong enough or heavy enough, and the wire sang and vibrated but did not loosen. The tears poured down my face, salty and warm on my lips. Hot sweat replaced cold. I screamed with despair and frustration and fright. It helped, so I did it again and again and again and went on screaming and kicking my legs in the dirt, my nose an inch from the dried faeces, till my legs were seized and I was dragged, shrieking with terror, back from the entrance into the scented bracken, where I was slapped hard on the naked thigh like a kid and rolled over to find Matthew staring at me, his eyes glittering in an ashen face. 'Are you hurt?' he asked.

I couldn't stop screaming until he yelled at me and

started to walk into the dolmen when I howled at him in frenzy. I told him what was in there, and what I had been trying to do. He was very quiet, leaned in, found the wire and pulled it up. The boulder thudded on to the earth floor. Panting in the sun I watched him. I didn't dare speak. I didn't know what to say. I had never seen a man frightened before, and he was not afraid of the boulder. Starkly he wound the wire up, collected the peg, and rolled the boulder out into the bare place from which Anna had taken it. There were white roots and shoots there, exposed, white and dank like intestines of interior worms. I was sick behind the stone, and then we started to walk back. I forgot my reservations about him and clung to his hand. Eventually he said, 'I'm sorry, Helen. That was my fault. I didn't know you were out.'

'YOUR fault?' I shrank from him, grabbing my hand from him—

'No, no. I don't mean it that way. I didn't know anyone was up here, and I thought I should take Anna back to the house before I came here to have a look round.' He spoke very matter-of-factly, his eyes on the sycamores just coming into view over the rise.

'You mean you knew what she had done?' I demanded, incredulously.

'No. I just thought she might have done something. I came to look.'

'Was it—who was it meant for?' He did not answer that but walked steadily on through the heather. I was nearly trotting to keep up with him. Unable to keep quiet I burst out, 'But it would have hurt the first person who went in. It could have been anyone, me, a kid from the cottages, anyone at all.'

'It was not,' he said slowly, 'an entirely responsible

action,' and looked down sideways at my horrified gasp. 'Anna is not an entirely responsible person.'

I thought, hell, she's not, she's a bloody nut case. Then I thought, Jesus, she IS a nut case. Really. I said, 'Matthew, is Anna mad?' and he said, 'NO. But limited in some aspects.' And my blood congealed about my hair roots and shrank away to the furthest inwardness of me, so that I was chill in the high sun, the only chill thing on the face of the bog.

'You will have noticed,' he went on, 'how she likes things to be neat. Disorder—distresses her.' He still was not looking at me.

I remembered the plate of cheese straws the very first evening that Anna had so anxiously reset, re-positioned, each time I cruelly took one from its appointed place in the pattern. I remembered how she danced with Peter, her pleasure in the form they made, not in the dance, not in the man. I remembered how she had brushed invisible hairs into place behind the dolmen. I began to shake again. 'She shouldn't be left alone,' I said desperately.

'She isn't, usually.' He looked at me now, uncertainly. 'I've said I am sorry.'

'And what, what on earth is it to do with you?'

'Haven't you guessed, Little Helen Wykham?'

But I hadn't guessed, and only shook my head dumbly at him. The bulk of the house was visible in the trees. Soon we must stop talking. Hurriedly I said, 'Tell me, Matthew. If you tell me I won't be frightened.' It was not true.

'I look after Anna. I have been looking after her for five years now. So far no one but you has had occasion to ask about her. I take the lesson, and I will be more careful and exercise greater discipline in future.'

At the quietness of his voice I moved a little further off into the side of the path. Now, I was afraid of him too. I do not like this word discipline, spoken softly.

'Does Dominic know? Does he? Matthew, have they told him, warned him?'

'Dominic knows as much as he needs to know. He is very careful. He is conducting the whole affair as elegantly as I knew he would.'

'You know him—I mean, knew him?'

'O, yes. I've known Dominic for years.'

We passed between the rhododendrons and drew close to the arch into the stable yard. He turned suddenly. 'Little Helen Wykham, you have guessed a great deal. But you don't know everything. Have mercy on us all, and keep these piteous doings to yourself.'

Dazed as a novice, I said, 'I will,' and watched him go away into the house through the library doors. His walk was that of an old man. O God, have mercy on us all. Have mercy.

◘

I endured supper in torment. We ate early because we were all going to the theatre in the evening. It was an hour's drive, more or less, into Dublin and so we were given Gentleman's Relish sandwiches and Christmas cake in the library before we set off. I couldn't make up my mind if it were last Christmas' or next Christmas'. Everyone was showing a regrettable tendency to pair up, which was making me feel relieved, because it meant that the people I was afraid of, like Dominic and Stephanie, and in a different way Anna, were catered for and occupied so that I could sit back and watch. It also depressed me, because with the Francis-Topsy alliance still enduring despite the disparity of intention exhibited by the participants, with Harriet as close to Bill as she could decently get (and he was not so decent), with Stephanie feeding Dominic on Gentleman's Relish while he sat in his familiar place on the piano stool apparently mending a light plug, which struck me as an odd thing to do at a party; with Matthew sticking to Anna like a warder, which apparently he was (to stop her putting arsenic in the Relish?) and Maria deep in worried and inebriated conversation with the French woman, in her allotted place by the fire, I was left over. So was Peter. I skedaddled off around the *National Geographic* and came into a cul-de-sac between Harriet's back and Matisse in three volumes. I peeped through the gap between them and saw Peter looking hurt. I immediately felt sorry, contrite and pure of heart, and sallied out. 'Hi!' I said, brightly. 'Haven't seen you all day.'

'What have you been doing?' he asked curiously, looking at the elastoplast where the wire had cut my finger.

'O, I stayed in bed, and then went off for a walk by myself,' I said, naïvely.

'Well, you would hardly have seen me, then, would you?'

O God. It just wasn't WORTH it. The amount of charity I had put into that remark, and all I got was sarcasm. I said, giving up, 'Ooh, well, I don't know. I might have,' and leered at him with my bottom lip wet and protuberant, like they do at the Gate when they play a tart.

'I don't know what you mean,' he muttered stiffly, adjusting his Old Wellingtonian tie.

'You've pushed it too far to the left,' I said. 'No, my left. Your right.' He couldn't help fiddling with it. His nostrils twitched angrily. I put my hand on his arm and gave it an ever-so-tiny squeeze. 'Smashing,' I said, as if I'd said, Come to my room later. I leered again and caught Stephanie's eye. She started to giggle. Dominic looked up, peeping between his floppy hair and the top rim of his spectacles, and his mouth moved in encouragement, but I was suddenly suffused with embarrassment by his eyes and looked away, giving Peter his chance to march off. I whistled *Shall we Gather at the River* very softly, but he heard me, and turning round on the stool, the plug on his knees and a screwdriver in his teeth, began to play it. I hid among Matisse and Harriet and listened. I didn't know one could be witty or catty on the piano. Peter failed to make the connexion and arrived up beside Stephanie who was eating Dominic's sandwich. Vastly encouraged I came out of hiding and joined them. Apart from the spasmodic gallop the night before, I had never been so close to him. I could smell that shaving stuff again. I could see down his collar; I could see his skin and his muscles; I saw why he held Loftus' reins wide and why his hands were strong; he stopped suddenly and flicked one leg back over the stool, so that I was caught gazing down at his mouth . . . his lips . . .

He said, 'Will you come in my car?'

Hypnotised, I said, 'Yes. If there is room,' and felt the blood starting out of all my major arteries.

'I wouldn't suggest it if there were not room. Steph, I am like to die of starvation; give me back my bun and when I am refreshed I will procure more. I have created a *coup d'état* in the kitchen by fixing an electric fan where they keep the food. This ought to prevent most of it from having to be thrown out before we get it, and thus ensure peace in the domestic regions, and plenty in the dining room. Hand over.' God, he was frail looking. Why did he always sit crooked like that, hunched, deformed almost?

She fed him, wee erotic movements to and from his tongue and teeth. Peter stood watching, his muscles jumping again. His knuckles were white. Stephanie turned to him, 'May I come with you?' she asked sweetly. What the hell, I thought.

He and Harriet had brought it over on the boat. It was a big, old fashioned tourer. The hood was down, and the breeze stirred the rugs and paper parcel in the back. I sat pressed against Matthew, because I was frightened by the roar and the speed of it and by being within a few inches of Dominic's back for an hour. Anna was sitting as far from him as she could get, pressed against the door, her face turned to the window. Before we started he had leaned across her and locked the door, and she had shrunk back as if he had been a loathsome thing. To me too, at this moment, blasting through the gorges, he seemed a fearful thing. Watching the way the wind blew his hair into curls behind his ears and into long silky skeins at the nape, which was so like Laurence's, I felt my whole precious being penetrated by his proximity. It was as if he dispersed within me all that was familiar and fought for and filled me instead with himself. He created that Helen within me which was only his, and which was but lightly touched by identity, so that I hated him a little and feared him greatly, likening him in my mind to the random expanse of disorder that had hurled the great blocks of stone down the shattered cliffs about us. The Scalp is a monstrous place; a gap knocked out of the mountains, where world-matter is tossed violently on each side, yet never moves. And curiously, it has a human significance too. On one side, the mountains and the bogs raise the earth to abstract and rare planes; on the other, almost immediately through the rift, the ribbon-building of the nation's capital claws its way up from the squamose bay, depositing its trivia and its melodrama, its rules and its vindictivenesses, almost within touching distance of the grand disorder strewn across its way. It was towards this that we were hurtling. This Dominic was driving us. I sought Matthew's hand under the rug, for fear was following me down from Calary. The hand went round mine nearly twice and overlapped on the other side.

'It's a constant wonder to me, this place,' Dominic said softly. I leaned forward to hear him, surprised to find so urbane a creature affected by this cold chaos. 'It's a hiatus in nature; between the moorland which owes nothing to the human eye and cares nothing for it and the tender gardens made by men for their explicit pleasure. A blank place. A rest. I like it.'

Neither Matthew nor Anna seemed surprised to hear him speak so. Anna said, 'Your car destroys its quiet,' and he nodded, conceding culpability. 'I know. I danced with a magnificent woman last week,—gosh, yes; well, anyway . . .' Matthew laughed.

'Shut up. She was telling me how she lived in a garden of roses and palm trees. I was just thinking—the antithesis of Calary.'

Gruffly I said, 'We live in a garden like that. All the

houses on the sea side in Dalkey grow roses and palms.'

'That was the place. It was strange—being with her was like the kissing of worlds; my hands, my clothes, all smelled of turf fires and peat water, three thousand years of rain and sky, and she smelled of luxurious oils and things made and exquisite.' He laughed suddenly. 'I spent the whole time refraining from sniffing her like a dog. Just for the wonder of it.' Anna's shadowy eyes glanced obliquely at him. I held on to Matthew. For her sake. 'I was thinking of it last night. There was a fire in the library—'

'You are supposed to go to bed at night,' Matthew said primly, 'not to contemplate nature. It is considered more normal than collecting the local flora all day and then sitting about consigning its ancestors to the flames all night. There is something sadistic in that. Not at all nice, is it, Helen Wykham, mine?'

But I was astonished. 'Do you collect flowers, Dominic?'

'Not really. I sit around and look at them. I seldom take them. Sometimes, of course, they take me in revenge, like when I fell off Loftus into a bog-pool immediately after stuffing my pockets with heather to take home.'

Anna said vaguely, 'Brendan was much impressed by your prowess, that day. So was Ma, of course.'

'Of course. My father was an excellent horseman,' he replied wryly.

'What was he really like, Dominic?' Matthew asked with that passionate inquisitiveness he had for strange people.

'Gerald? Me.'

'Not to look at.'

'Oh. Oh—I can't tell you, Matthew. Hell, I was fifteen by the time he came back from wherever he had been.

127

I lived with him for a year. I don't know what he was like. I adored him—beyond idolatry. I can't tell you. But I can tell you that he wouldn't have spent his life sitting about looking at flowers and reading history books, which is how I spend my—endless time.'

I thought, Why should your petty hobbies be the passions of my life?

Without emphasis Anna said, 'Since you like history so much you should walk up behind the house. There is a dolmen there—it would interest you.'

Among the laburnums and the tall, hypocrytical conifers of those Dublin suburbs where those of us lived who didn't live in Dalkey, Fear caught up with and overtook us. But Dominic did not notice it passing us. He was murmuring to himself, ' . . . *among the heath and hare bells, listened to the soft wind breathing through the grass . . .*'

Outraged, I snapped, 'Harebells grow on the chalk.'

'Don't blame me, blame Emily—'

'Harebells grow on chalk.' I couldn't let him take that, my harebells, turn them black with his touch, his grave-pit fingers—

'That's what I am saying,' he said softly. Not to me.

'NO!' I had been there. I had told lies, faced expulsion, to get there, up to the high white chalk where Lyn lived and walked among the harebells and the orchids that shadowed the grass where no shade was . . .

'Heath and harebells, heath and harebells, heath and harebells . . .' he shouted insistently, as if it meant something.

I think there was movement in the car; his shouting was so savage, so sudden. 'I went on a bus ride once,' I explained stiffly, as if to a stubborn child, 'from Salisbury, through Amesbury and Durrington, and—Durrington—

and—' wherefore could I not pronounce Upavon?

'I know where that bus goes.'

'Upavon,' I said.

'Upavon,' he said.

◨

Then he said, 'Do you know Upavon?' and his voice
was as if in the wilderness he were asking for water. It
was a cold wilderness, full of rocks and dust, like they
now tell us the moon is. I knew. I was in it with him.

'I knew someone there once,' I said, and he said,
'So did I, once.' He made a strange empty gesture with
one hand and the car rushed through the wide streets,
under warm Georgian façades, as it had been a wilderness
or Nagasaki. Once I had had a dream of Mother walking
down this very street, her heels tapping on the pavement
as she passed under the tall wrought gas standards; and
as she passed, each standard lit and the wide fanlights
sprang into golden relief. I had woken crying. But in the
driving mirror Dominic's eyes were as still as the cold
iron doors of a vault beyond which dead men or great
riches lie, and I had nothing to give him, and no lights
lit for us as we passed. I leaned my head on the door and
spoke her name into the wind, that it might take her
away from me forever into its mindless force.

◨

I stood on the side of the road watching the cars in
the street while Dominic pulled the hood up and locked
the doors of the tourer. I noticed that they veered about
in their lanes and rushed as if they might achieve some-

thing, like knocking someone down or getting a drink
before the chap in the Austin behind. I noticed how alike
their shapes were and how patternless; they could be
going backwards or forwards, and only the colour of the
lights would tell you. Dominic, his hands in his pockets,
was staring at Red Hugh's tower as if he had forgotten
where we were going and was speculating on going into
the Castle instead. We had had some difficulty in directing
him to the theatre; he seemed suddenly unable to tell his
right hand from his left, or red lights from green.
Matthew called his attention to the theatre lights, but
he went back three times to the car, for his glasses, for
the tickets, and finally because he had left the keys in the
ignition. Anna stood politely by, watching him. He did
not seem to be aware of any of us and swore steadily and
obscenely to himself as he journeyed to and from the
edge of the pavement. Finally he looked at the three of
us, waiting by the No Parking sign and said, 'I am so
sorry. Shall we go and have a drink? We seem to be in
front of the others,' and the effort of this courtesy was
so great in him that sweat started out on his top lip.
I stood by, inept, merciless, impatient for him to come
out of his sickness so that he should drag me out of mine.
I had not time nor energy to watch others suffer. I felt
it inconsiderate of circumstances to produce enigmas and
miseries when my very life was threatened by enigma
and misery. I glared angrily at Dominic. He looked away.
'Come,' he said, and four sets of little secrets moved
discreetly across the road.

It was evening. The pubs were open. A tinker or two
lingered about the doors. The street stank of beer and
stout. Noise and laughter and an occasional shout drifted
through the ventilators in the frosted windows, emerging

mangled, violent and meaningless from the blades. I bumped into Dominic's back. Unaccountably he had stopped in front of the bar door. We couldn't go in THERE! But he was fumbling in his pocket. He pulled out a handful of small change and looked at it. The tinker was almost as tall as he was; a great raw-boned wench, up from the West. She wore the uniform of her station, the tatty petticoat and fringed rug. Her legs were bare and hairy. She did not move but stood against the tiled doorway with her hand out. Their eyes were level and both pairs very black. A man from within pushed them apart coming out, and stumbled away down the pavement. Returning, the tinker and Dominic were closer than before. They seemed to know each other very well, accepting each other's eyes on the grey Dublin corner. Mutely his hand repeated her gesture, open as if to receive. Their sight was shared, and everything was very still. Slowly Adam put his gift back in his pocket and drew a five pound note from his wallet instead. He smoothed it carefully between his fingers before he gave it to her, and taking it Eve turned and went through the swing doors of the pub, leaving Adam outside in the evening.

◻

The fine movement had been troubling the corner of my eye for some time. I leaned over a little to look as Stephanie turned from the gaudy stage to watch him in the dark. His arm moved at her gesture. He was trembling all over, like a stricken dog. During the second act he left his seat and vanished from the theatre.

The play over, searching for him we found him sitting quietly in his car, fine black hairs on the shoulder of his grey suit. Harriet drove him home to Calary Bog.

Letter xlvii

My sweet love,

    Now that the moment of donation has arrived and I see that I have no gift, I am relieved of all responsibility and find myself quite gay and happy. I had thought to present you with a portrait of the person I had imagined myself to be in those uncertain days before the events which I am about to relate had scarred the features. But now I find that there was no such person, and so I can offer only a featureless cartoon. There are no scars. I see that the development of my love for Lyn, the existence of Dominic, and the fact of Laurence, superimposed upon the cartoon those forms which exist and which have successively been called my individuality and recognised as me.

    Loving Lyn was my first existence as an individual, so that in a sense it is she who is really my mother. I was brought forth out of that love ignorant of its true significance as a baby is ignorant of the fact of its birth. And like an infant I accepted and utilised faculties and features as they became identifiable. It is not the child who begets the man or the man who engenders the child but the paramour who is mother to both. My contact with her formed an aspect of myself which could only be produced by her. It is a mark of my malleability that the lines are still there for you to comment on. They are the first cast of my features; I was mistaken to think them scars. Other acts, other loves have imposed their several identities, yours by no means the least happy of them. There has been no act of volition on my part in the creation of this Helen peculiar to you.

    Thus, my sweetest love, I have reduced myself quite away. I am just a nonsense of features designed by the love-dreams of others, and no wonder I feel gay and irresponsible. Bear with me.

    But, Aileen, I cannot quite reduce Lyn to a nonsense. Not even now.

Helen

'I think you ought to go home,' Stephanie said, awkwardly. 'I thought I'd ring Mother, and ask her to fetch you. O.K.?'

I said, 'NO. Not O.K. at all. I want to stay,' but when she asked why, showing more wit than I would have given her credit for, I had no answer. So instead I said, 'You're sleeping with him, aren't you?' and she answered, 'Jesus. I wish to God I wasn't,' and began to cry for the first time for years.

I didn't know what to say then, either. She looked ugly on my crumpled bed, her bottom lip sticking out and her nose dribbling while the tears belched out of her, and she twisted the sheet into limp, damp ropes.

After a while I asked, 'He's not—not beastly to you, is he?' wondering if she would know that I knew what I meant. But she didn't notice and only cried harder, saying that he was scrupulously polite and considerate, and that she'd never been with anyone so good at it in her life, and that he did things that used to make her feel sick when she read about them but which were like all the joys of Paradise with him.

I didn't actually know what all that was about, but I was quite willing to use my imagination and believe her. 'What's wrong, then?' I asked, now rather lost. But I had broken the spell of confidence with my tone, and she began to sniff and make shifts towards pulling herself together.

'It's a bit difficult to explain, but I would like to feel he thought I was nearly human, or even sub-human,' she said, with an effort at tartness. 'I might as well be a bottle of wine or an outsized sleeping pill.'

I grinned at her, and to my intense surprise she suddenly grinned back.

'Like you said, all fraught emotions and sexual currents,' and I laughed because I had forgotten I had said that and because it seemed to be fun to talk to Stephanie, suddenly, since I had told Dominic about the bus to Upavon. So I said, tentatively, 'You don't, well, LIKE him or anything, do you?' But she said, 'Good God, no,' and I believed her, realising that all she was after was a way out of the obligations of his personality, and of keeping right on with the joys of Paradise. So I said indignantly, 'You ought to fall in love; it'd do you good.'

And she laughed at me, saying, 'See who's talking! Sure, but not with Dominic. All he wants out of life is a series of nice hair-raising sex-sensations to take his mind off whatever it's on. Being sick, I suppose, and not being a pianist any more, or whatever he was. And I don't fancy myself as an alternative to a dose of Epsom salts.'

'I'm not sure that you don't.' My previous failed conversation, rearing its romantic head in my mind, made me cross. I knew she wouldn't take advice from me. I wasn't sure that I wanted to give it any more. Let her treat him like a whore would, I thought. The way they both carried on, I reckoned, it was their fault anyway. I muttered, 'If you stopped being a whore, people might stop thinking of you as one—' but something in her eyes stopped me from saying any more because all she was after was a sort of Paradise where you got one sensation between the legs and another in the heart, and I thought there was not much difference in their attitudes, just that they were applied to different people, which could be considered rather a pity. I said, 'There's no point in wanting to mother Dominic, he might commit incest,' and got the slap that she had reserved for Peter. I deserved it.

134

It was a morning of home truths all right, because when I was rubbing my cheek she shouted, 'The trouble with YOU is that you're queer as a coot, as well as ignorant and cold as a fish.'

'You ought to do zoology, you'd make terrific discoveries,' I sneered, and she slammed out of the door. I had my turn crying, rolling about on the bed and making a really good job of it, so that everyone would know I had a raw deal. Which, with one thing and another, I had. But it didn't get me any further with Stephanie. Maybe I had hoped to reclaim her lost virtues, or something. But I think I was only jealous. It was she who had made the only point in the interview. That it showed. I wondered how long she had known it; longer than I had.

As you will have realised by now, I am not athletic. I am not the sporty type, nor am I team spirited. One of the reasons why I am not team spirited is that I am so unsporty that no one ever wanted me in her team, so I got used to thinking that teams were a bind anyway. I used to stand in nice, solitary places by the hedge during games at school and had discovered an extraordinary, efficient method of removing my presence from the consciousness of the gym mistress. Because I rode (or maybe for another reason, but that doesn't matter here), I had outrageously strong thighs and had discovered in my Third Form days that I could hang upside down on the top of the parallel bars for an indefinite length of time. Getting me up was enough to impress the mistress that I was present and functioning gymnastically, and there I would remain for thirty-five minutes, motionless, forgotten, perfectly happy upside down in my blue woolly knickers, while everyone else galloped about behaving like ballerinas in a junk yard or pigs trying for Becher's Brook, according to their temperament and ability.

I now put this convenient talent to good use. I was hanging from a rather slender bough of one of the larches which the Forestry Commission had decided were in for our generation, halfway up an Irish mountain, admiring the way the leaves or needles grew in bunches on their own little stalks. It was rather a scraggy apology for a tree, and I thought that if I were as scrawny as that, *I* wouldn't be deciduous for all the needles on the Weymouth Pine. I became quite dreamy, tucked in there against the corrugated trunk, thinking of some of Daddy's better efforts, when his clients had let him get away with it, and how he had taught me to love the plants and their long, exotic names. Even when we passed the common ash tree, he used to say, '*Fraxinus excelsior*, the most beautiful name for the most beautiful tree,' and told me how the ancient Greeks had thought Cupid's bow to be made of ash. He was a nice man, my dad; a bit unrealistic, but nice. He had told me, too, that the larch was not a native of these islands but a Tudor introduction, like the turkey, and I thought, 'How like them, turkeys and larches,' and a fat lot of sympathy I had for either. Especially now. And that furthermore it had been a jolly silly idea of Topsy's to make a whole lot of pseudo-adults trot round a wood playing hide-and-seek, with the instant result that Topsy cheated and found Francis, Bill cheated and found Harriet, and Stephanie didn't even bother to cheat but walked off with her hand tucked into the band of Dominic's trousers. So all round the wood, Matthew, Anna, or possibly Matthew-and-Anna combined, the French woman, Peter and I were assiduously avoiding all the places where a couple might hide, or each other might lurk, lest we be immediately compromised and branded as Scarlet for the rest of our social lives. Hence I was upside down in a *Larix decidua* half way up a mountain, as I have said.

Well, the inevitable happened, as you will have guessed, or the whole incident, otherwise so trivial, would have gone unrecorded. My beautiful sister and her botanical paramour came idling into the scrappy shade of the larches, in quest, no doubt, of Paradise. I discovered that if I craned my neck backwards so that my soles tickled the back of my double crown I could watch them. It is neither a posture nor a viewpoint which I could recommend with any honesty to an aspiring Peeping Tom, and as for providing a chapter in my sexual education it was not a thundering success. I overheard a great many remarks which could not conceivably make sense and was scandalised to find at one stage that Dominic had lit a cigarette and was lying there, puffing away on top of my poor sister. Poor sister did not seem to mind much, and I wondered if this made the grade to the Pearly Gates. From my angle it looked frankly boring, and I watched the sequentia with great interest and mounting ambivalence until they sat up and started dressing themselves; Stephanie with great attention to detail, and Dominic much more haphazardly, due to the harvest of needles he had garnered in his underpants, which were of a startling red and green design with leaping race horses in unseemly places. This afforded Stephanie vast amusement; me, too. Then they went away, complacently entwined about each other, just as they had come, and I was left dangling fifteen feet up from the scene of their ecstasy.

All in all, I was a bit shocked. I had read that you did do this sort of thing in broad daylight, and of course the German songs and Greek myths were full of it, but this was a bit close to home. And any one might have seen them—me for instance. Did they not mind? Or did they presume that everyone else was similarly occupied— me for instance? Nor did I like the little sounds of bliss. They reminded me of nasty things—wrack in the rock clefts in a lifting tide, Anna in the dolmen. Tiny, intimate, nasty things. I thought intimacy was a nasty word, a dirty word. I thought that if Anna did not feel kindly towards Dominic, intimacy might be a very dirty word indeed to her. I came down from my larch, isolated and very lonely because I had not enjoyed what I had seen, and it had been the opportunity of my life and one which I had scarcely admitted to myself that I had been waiting for. So my unhappiness was very great, and I did not want to think of Dominic for a long time to come. And I thought, This will never change, whatever else may. I will always be the other side of pleasure. This was dismaying. I leaned against the trunk in the pale green light for a long time before I went in search of the French woman, who was baking potatoes in the embers of the fire. 'Caught,' I said sulkily, touching her shoulder.

'Entirely caught.' She didn't look up but grabbed my wrist and pulled me down on the path beside her. 'My foolish cousin said it was safe to have builded the fire in the path where there are no trees, and that he would be back to keep an eye upon it, but he is not come back.'

'Built,' I said, automatically. 'He'll be here soon. He has just finished making love to my sister under the larch trees up there, so he won't be long.'

I could see the parting in her tightly drawn hair and thought what a clean scalp she had. I wondered if Dominic would wash his hands before he ate his potato . . .

'And do you mind?' she enquired politely. I thought about this for a minute.

'No,' I said eventually. 'No, I don't mind, really.' Somehow it seemed a natural conversation. The smoke went up very straight from the fire, and what voices we could hear were a long way off. The potatoes smelled sweet and made my mouth runny, so that I swallowed noisily in the hot quiet.

'Were you watching?'

'Yes. I saw bits of it.' I stared at the ruts in the path. I knew she was not looking at me.

'Did he look like this?'

I stared at her, suddenly. Something queer happened to her mouth and to the sides of her nose; her bottom lip altered, I could see her tongue . . .

I shrieked with laughter—'O yes, yes exactly like that —exactly—O God, DO stop!' But she went on and on till my sides hurt, and she began to laugh too, and we rolled in idiot malice in the path with tears of merriment on our cheeks at Dominic's expense. Then we sat up and looked at each other, and the giggling bubbled in my throat and spilled out in the forest, and every time she looked up from poking the spuds she twitched her face into superb mockery and once scratched her groin, so I told her about the larch needles in his racy knickers, and she yelped with delight till Matthew came to see what was going on and found us rocking, crosslegged by the fire, with the spuds charring gently in the sunlight. But she became quiet then and would not come down off her dignity to giggle in front of Matthew and Anna. And Anna sat like a little, pale idol in the aqueous light, her hands folded in her lap. And one by one, they all came back—it seems that it takes all sorts about the same statutory twenty-five minutes—and he came and sprawled on his back, considerably more than half asleep, and every time he fidgeted his hips or his bottom she looked at me, and I felt like bursting into a shower of sparks, thinking of the scaly pricking in his pants. And I despised him utterly, wriggling his thin buttocks in the earth, with his eyes shut against the drifting sun and smoke, utterly beautiful in the summer. Ding-dong, don't wake him up . . .

Don't wake him up, for he is most beautiful asleep, all intelligence erased, and only magic in the bone, in the ignorant calcareous structures. How the sun vivifies and informs, making so passionless that which is passionate, so wonderful that which dare not wonder. How easeful, and slight the light of *Larix decidua* upon the dead, and the absent, and the sleeping, who are, after all, more or less the same. Slight light also on my head, I who am now present, though formally absent, grave and observant, quiescent in the forest light. Nascent in the forest light. Such existence is an undertaking so grievous and so wayward that only the ritual of sleeping confines it and confirms it. Infants sleep as he does, and drunks, and the mortally injured. How am I now an infant in this world, this violent, noiseful, brilliant world, and sleep by his side, sleeping one, absent one, dead another. Don't wake him up, let him dream on of the time before injury, and I at his side of the time after birth . . .

So it was that in the pale sub-light I stretched out beside him and put my head down in my arms beside her knees and slept while the potatoes grew cold and the dreams warmed my cold little heart and empty thighs. In my sleep I prayed to a receding God not to let my mother know that I had grown up at last.

'Look, look, Helen.'

I opened my eyes lazily into the day. 'What?'

Francis held the smooth root out to my eyes. Smooth with the slime of burial, white with burial, suddenly exposed to my destructive sight. Why choose me? Why my eyes? 'See, it's a Madonna . . .'

WHY TELL ME?

Dominic stirred and looked, but he said nothing, a great silent Nothing into the silence in which Topsy sat and stared. It was a beginning—

LAURENCE

I WAS THE White Hart from Bordeaux stalking the corridors of Sheen; I was Rufus and Richard pausing for the necessary moment in the King's New Forest for the bow to aim; I was Oldcastle opening his lips for the great first vowel of prayer on the Cheapside, the grey rain of the Marches already damping down his hair; I was Job, constipated with starvation, wondering when Rex Angelorum would send the haemorrhoids; I was Isaac face down on the hastily heaped bed of boulders, heels to his father's expectant face; I was a limb of Satan; I was not a limb of Satan, I was the arse-hole of Lucifer. I was wearing a blue velvet housecoat which did not suit me at all and which I adored. I was standing still on those perpetual stairs that run up the house on Calary like a dildo in an ignorant hand, turned this way and that and put to futile uses. It was not dark when I stood half way along the dildo, because the first floor landing lights were on. There was no music tonight. But there were sounds, like Isaac would have made, or Job, if the sacrifice or the trial had ever actually happened. And yet not quite like that. There is a very, very slight difference between the grunts of extreme pain and the grunts of extreme passion. Very slight. But distinguishable, though similarly effective in making the belly clench and the hair scratch between the legs of the listener.

Maria was standing outside his door, a dusty bottle of cognac in her hand. She was wearing men's dungarees strapped over yellow spotted pyjamas, so that her unrestrained tits bulged out on either side of the wide straps, useless, misplaced. A cigarette hung from her lip, and she was twisting a corkscrew into the top of the bottle while she listened to his grunts. She was tremendously concentrated, twisting faster as the bed began to creak and the tempo of noise increased. When the cork was out of the bottle-neck Maria bowed her head, thrust the loaded corkscrew into her pocket and knocked at the door. After a long time she knocked again. The opening of the door revealed a man's angry face against the brighter light from within, part of the great double bed and Dominic's left leg from thigh to ankle. It was crooked and quivering. Above the sound Maria said, 'His uncle was always given this. Up the ass.' She handed the bottle in through the crack in the door. 'You can have the funnel we fill the petrol cans with. If you like, that is.'

'Thank you, Lady Calary. I have all the necessary equipment. I don't think that will be needed. But if you could find an electric bar or radiator, and some more towels, old ones . . . ?'

When the door shut in her face she wiped her mouth on her pyjama sleeve and turned to the stairs. 'Bloody fool. Thinks he knows more about this than I do. Bloody fool. Gerald, Thomas, Uncle Benedict—all had brandy up like that. Napoleon for old Unk, no doubt. Bloody fool. That Helen? Come here, child, I need a hand. That bloody fool in there won't give the boy brandy. Call himself a doctor. Only just out of the maternity ward himself—saw milk on his chin! Ha—thinks we have electric fires. Will you help me collect the turf and some sticks? Anna's locked up with that Laurence. No sense of reality that girl. I'll get the vet next time; he knows what it's all about, does old Pat.'

She drew me down the stairs simply by dint of going on talking, and I was not able to turn rudely away. '—Or do it myself, but he's strong, and I'm getting older now. They used to sit on the old man's head to keep

146

him down. Bit Dominic's grandmother in the bum once he did, at sixty-eight, right through her petticoats, so it bled, and every tooth that did it his own. We can light the fire with a paraffin rag, if Grogan hasn't used it all on the dog's ticks. Great men in our family. Mind the step down, lovey, it's dark down here, and not too even. Great men, but dry in the bowels. I didn't know the boy was so bad till he got over here. If you hold that sack open at the neck, I'll heave the turf in; you won't want to dirty that pretty blue costume.' In the light of the 40-watt bulb, breasts dangling past the coarse braces, she took a huge flat shovel from the cellar floor and started to fill the sack. Shivering I held the mouth wide. The sack was rough and cool to the touch. Turf dust settled about the hessian. 'His sister's drinking like a bishop in the kitchen. No bloody use at all. Scared to death of him, if you ask me. And she with a babe and everything—ought to be used to the stink of a man by her age. How do I know? Saw her belly serving on the tennis-court last week. Silly shorts and blouses they wear these days, can't hide a thing like a recent birth on the tennis court. Not serving overarm. And that Francis sicking up all over the Afghan rug, he'll get over it, if the boy doesn't die too soon. Nothing like martyrdom to provide eternal life. There, that's as much as we'll carry between us. Bring that shelf there and I'll chop it for sticks. Quicker than Grogan or Brendan. Bloody hatchet's blunt as a bollard. You're not afraid of spiders, are you? Hop up on the anvil, there, you won't damage it. Have to get an outside smith these days. Forty bob a pair, without studs.'

Perched on the anvil; one eye on the spider heading for me; other eye on Maria's rippling forearm swinging the hatchet, heavy as a bollard. Sweat about the anus, malformations of the finger joints and ulna. Giant shadows leaping around the once whitewashed walls as the splintering began and the brackets came off the pale green once-shelf. Weight of the house squatting above me, evacuating its lumpy secrets into my watery brain.

'—But if the boy doesn't breed he's the last of that line, and we ought to get out of it. Heir is only a second cousin, and they've married out now for two generations. No sign of the sickness but they're soft in the head, not like the boy at all. He's bright enough, God knows. And could woo Gabriel with his music, like his uncle—the one that went under the 7.47 for Rugby at Tring cutting. Wrote psalm settings. S.J., of course, like Francis will be. The boy and that friend of his were singing them the other night, before you all came; like Paradise it was, and the boy so like Gerald. Thought I'd got over hearing my heart crack or at least got deaf to it, but it seems not. There is some paraffin—that means I'll have to check the dogs myself, again. Fourteen on Biddy last year, after they said they'd done. Cigarettes are the best things; burn their asses and they pop out to see what's going on, and you get them with a tweezers. I told that Nuala to see that there was always a fire in his room, but like hell she'll come down here. Only time she ever did, I forced her to it by having no fire in the house—here, you take the sticks and that corner, and I'll take this side— who'd have thought old heather and moss would be so heavy?—heave her up that step and I'll do the light with my chin—the boy was on at me for wasting money on the bloody electricity. Then he fits up an electric fan in the larder that goes off of its own accord and puts out the hall lights. My father would die in his grave if he thought the door was not lit in welcome all night. Had no heat in the house all one January till that Nuala came down and brought up sticks. Gerald used to have a big coat with sheepskin lining to it; brown, with straps for keeping it out of the way of your stirrup leathers, and we used to put that on him in bed when he was sick, and even then his nose dribbled. But I don't suppose baby-face in there would stand for that. 'Unhygienic,' he'd say, I bet, and it was a hot thing full of sweat and oil, warm as your own hairs. Wait here now while I find a rag to put the paraffin on. What's this?'

'Stephanie's headscarf,' I said numbly. Stairs only two yards away—can hear the sounds from here—

'You have to pay for your pleasures someway, I was taught. She can give him this to keep him warm, he's been keeping her warm enough in all conscience. Come on, then, we'll drag it up. You go on the bannister side and you can pull on them . . . good girl, there's a lot of your mother's spirit in you. You're the only one around to give a hand, and not puking. You'd better not. come in, though, it may be a bit messy in there by now and you're only a child. Ever seen a man naked? Thought not—and this is not the way to find out—you go and get Laurence to give you a hand finding towels or an old sheet. Any old thing will do; she lives in there. Matthew will help with this, sent from God, straight from God, with an Apostle's name . . . do you want a fire or don't you? Here's turf and sticks, and I'll get it going in a minute while you would be wondering how to switch it on. Out of my way—I've seen him and his uncles and his father and his grand-father as God made them. I've brought you a fire, boy; tell him, Matthew—' and the door shut, this time on me. But I had had my eyes screwed shut in any case, so it made no difference. Or nearly, after I had seen the mess and his face and Matthew leaning on his upper arms and heard the sounds close to .' . . .

There was no one in the room next door. I found Laurence and Anna in the library. Of course the piano stool where he usually sat was empty. Bill was lying in a chair, his feet on four years of *The Horse and Hound*.

'They want old towels, or something,' I said, brushing turf off my skirts so that I need not look at her. I felt her look at me.

'Is he better?' Bill asked from under his brows. He struggled upright, and I saw that he had been sleeping. It was nearly five-thirty and getting light.

Hesitantly I replied, 'It's a bit messy and noisy in there still—' and he sighed deeply, rubbing his jaw. No one said anything for a moment, and Laurence began to uncurl stiffly from her chair. She looked uneasily from Anna to Bill and then at me. Her eyes were guarded, almost like Dominic's. The flutterings left my knees and began in my belly. Very deep in, further in than can be seen . . . I craved her thin shoulder for my eyes, her clean hair for my rigid cheeks, craved and craved so that I shook, and craved, to hide in her, recoil into her, to drive into her, by this action driving him out the other where, where he should not have ever been. She was not beautiful after a sleepless night, gritty and lined about the eyes, her hands sticky when she rubbed them on her skirt. I could feel my own nipples and an unlocalised ache somewhere about the pubic bone while he grunted and might die in the messy bed for lack of towels, for all things were crisis and heavy and fast with the momentum he had put upon them, and the absence of daytime in a room crowded with his absence, and nothing anywhere in the room or about the people in the room had any beauty whatsoever, not even by accident, as is so often so.

Laurence said, 'The towels are in the kitchen, in the big cupboard. Harriet is also in the kitchen, with the whiskey bottle.' She too sighed, brushing a membrane of restraint out of the air between us, exposing her tedium, her fatigue to me, like a stripper after the show. Loose flesh pricked irregularly over my arms.

'I'll come,' I offered, not even surprised that I understood, nor that she should accept my understanding, receive it as due, with no comment.

'Anna?'

In the end we all went, because Bill did not want to leave Harriet to our merciless contempt, and Laurence was with Anna, chained to Anna every second of day and dream time, nightmare Anna whose face was blank and pastel like magnolia caught in the frost and who walked docile and soft beside us in her diminutive felt slippers, her ears pointed to listen for the change in sound between a man living in agony and a man dying in agony. It even crossed my mind that she had indeed put arsenic in the Gentleman's Relish, or in the baked potatoes, or on the larch needles, and I wondered at this great feat of justice, that he should be brought to such a pass while Stephanie, who would not have puked either, was asleep; while Francis was asleep; while Peter, who would have enjoyed his humiliation, was asleep; and I, revelling in it, thought of lust; while Harriet was drunk and incapable; while Anna shrivelled and died with expectation; but Laurence, who didn't care and who had mocked him by the fire, fetched towels for Maria who had tried to sell him a wife. And I saw a great sorrow in the justice that inspired this shape; and then I saw it was not a justice but just a

shape. It was the shape of his love, Harriet, sitting on the
draining-board of the sink, methodically shelling peas and
hiccupping. It was the shape of her words, dancing
across the kitchen floor, in the parallel lines of the
stave, barring us off, line upon space upon line, '—a
second class love—a second class love. That's all we
are, just a pair of non-fucking, second class loves—' and
no clef to give us guidance.

I began the motions of making us coffee. Laurence
went upstairs with the linen from the big, ragged pile
in the cupboard. Anna brought mugs, aligning them
carefully along the edge of the deal table, handles at
right angles to the boards. I was uneasy and unsure of
how much Bill knew. I did not know if it were by accident
or design that he was sitting on the edge of the table
between Anna and Harriet, but I was glad he was there.
Nightmare Anna with her hands folded in her lap, staring
at Harriet across the mugs and the chipped milk jugs,
and Harriet staring back, her fingers green from the
pea-pods. In my bones the loss of Laurence was sharper
than a physical danger. I could not bear to see her in
my bright morning mind, up there near him. Though
they had the same name.

Bill said into the pale silence, 'He's much worse,
isn't he?'

And Anna replied. 'He will die soon,' she said.

'You've no bloody right to say that!' he snapped,
careless of her stillness.

'I have. I know he will. Won't he, Harriet?' Her
eyes did not flicker. A thread drew them tight across the
quarry tiles, tight to each other.

'Shut up Anna. It may not be true. And don't go at
Harriet . . . damn you—' he stood up, his bony wrists

twitching under his jersey, a conventional response. I heaped in the coffee.

Anna laughed, a little glass sound. 'What do you know about it? You don't like us all sitting round, thinking, will he die this time, or do we have to sit up another night and he'll do it at his leisure. You're a coward. Harriet wants him to die, don't you, Harriet?'

'No she doesn't. Shut up, will you. You're a hard little bitch. You mightn't care for him, but we do, Harriet and me. We love him. We know him—'

'Know HIM? Know the Dominic? Nobody knows him. Nobody wants to. He'll die, and we will all be free of him, won't we Harriet?'

'SHUT UP, ANNA!' Bill moved at her, as if he might touch her. Harriet sat very stiff, her feet in the sink, tied to Anna by the little thread. Bill tried to break it, flapping his hands in the air between them, as if he knew something was there.

'Stop it, Bill,' Harriet said. She bent her long, dark head over the peas and picked another pod from the tin basin. The dawn light strengthened behind her, eradicating her features and those of the pale Busy Lizzie in the pot on the window sill. The light quivered a little, afraid of violence. The violence was in Bill, in his arms and his jerking fists. It was not in any of us women. Because we were women, or about to be, it was not in us. Not even in me. We accepted it, pacific under it, archetypal in reaction, as Bill was too, who would go up and beat the pain or the death out of Dominic because he thought he loved him. Eventually Harriet spoke again. She spoke along the thread to Anna. 'Yes. He will die soon. Before the year is over, perhaps. You have nothing to worry about. And nothing to hurry over.'

'Jesus wept! I don't understand you, either of you! Two girls, just sitting there, and that poor bugger up there—Christ. Helen, give me some coffee. I'm going out in the yard, I can't listen to this, this . . . HARRIET why do you behave like this?'

'Stop it, Bill,' she said again. Then, 'Poor Bill, this isn't your department at all. Go to bed and sleep. Lauric will be all right in the morning.'

'It IS the morning. Lots of sugar, Helen, lots more.'

Laurence came in, her person beside me over the stove stronger than the thread, so that I could no longer see it but felt as if a door had been closed between me and some cold, raw weather in another place. In her interior comfort I grew bigger again and felt the plenitude that had been lost from the room while the two women and the man had spoken together. She told how Dominic was now better, asleep; Matthew and the doctor and Maria in need of coffee. She commended me for my foresight, gave Bill a tray and sent him upstairs as far as the landing with it. She asked Harriet if this were the usual pattern of events and seemed satisfied that it was. She moved deftly and sweetly among the crockery, over and around the thread, winding it up, closing the episode. She took Anna away to bed, giving her hot milk, accepting her renewed docility, treating her as a child who has been too long laughing.

When she had gone Harriet slid from the draining board. She came across the room to me, and I backed away a fraction, afraid of spells she might weave. But she only held out her hand and eventually I took it. 'I'm sorry,' she said. 'You didn't want to know any of that, did you?'

'No.'

Her eyes were enormous in her long face, far, far too big to ignore. 'Please don't be cross with me. I've said I'm sorry.'

'I'm not cross,' I said awkwardly.

'Yes, you are. Hold my hand. I can't bear Anna knowing that I want him to be dead. Verry was shot; bang-bang; Verry dead.' She made an urchin's gesture—two fingers projecting from the fist. 'In the Army. But Laurie is taking years—and I love him—I'm afraid the love won't last long enough.' She stared at our hands, clasped in front of us, as if she could find meaning in the gesture. 'Like Anna said, isn't it; how many nights do you have to sit up, waiting, when you've done it so many times for no reason, how often must you go on doing it? It's not as if there was any reason for sitting about, not as if there were any hope.' She stopped, lulled by her own words. 'I was trying to imagine what it would be like without him. But I can't even do that. I can't make schemes or preparations, because I can't believe in it. You can't prepare for something that doesn't exist. There are no references. So I get drunk. He gets cross with me too, but what else can I do?'

She seemed to want an answer, but I could only look at her miserably, because I could think of nothing for her to do and was also remembering the look of tedium on Laurence's face when I had told her that it was still all going on. I had an inspiration in which I understood about the love not lasting out the waiting. It seemed more terrible than anything I had yet seen.

Hypnotically she dragged on. 'He's so simple, really, no matter what Anna says. Dreadfully simple. And all this emotion is a muddle. Like Bill, all frenzy and affection and hypocritical fear, but we can't help it. But he's so appallingly simple—it seems wrong somehow—'

'Maria's not like that,' I said at last, 'nor Matthew, nor Anna. They are simple about it.'

'Naturally,' she said bitterly. She turned away and I let her hand go with relief. 'They are all simple-minded. Maria thinks it is the will of God or Someone. Matthew is a saint and all saints are simple-minded, and Anna's fit to be locked up. She looks daft. All that purity and malice, I bet she's just a half wit under it all.' She poked her hair behind her ear, and took a mug of half cold coffee. 'She has no reason to worry about being made to marry Laurie. Laurie won't marry anyone, and even if he got better by some miracle, which he won't, he'd not marry anyone against her will.' She was calm now and almost rational, a worried girl, the harridan fading out with the whiskey. She just wanted to talk. So she talked about Verry, whose name had really been Oliver, whom she hadn't married because she didn't believe in marriage. I told her about Mother and the step-fathers in return. Then she talked about Bill, whom she would learn to love, not as in the wild wonderful nights with Verry, but slowly. She did not talk at all about Dominic, whom she had always loved. I did not tell her any more.

When she had run dry, she said, 'Well, I'm going to bed now. There are lots of ghosts in it, but not Laurie's, thank God. But watch out in the morning. I'm tight, remember, so don't remind me of a single word I've said.'

After she had gone I washed the mugs. Then I dried them. Then I watered the Busy Lizzie. I sat on the table. Then I sat on the other side of the table. I put the kettle on. When it boiled I took it off again. I sat on the end of the table.

I left when I heard Doreen clattering down the bare servants stairs behind the dado.

There was no one in the hall; no one on the landing; no one in my bed.

◙

How matronly she was that morning! With superb dignity she rolled across the sky; with infinite ease and infinite leisure sliding into the first pale embrace of her lord, the Sun. All her waters flowed out from black to silver, and in her calm assurance exposed to his tender strength the most minute of all her desires, made timorous by night. Filled with wonder, I watched the earth turn into the sun's caress, as the gold moved across the pre-green wall, turning the paper and the plaster into a very garden. The last night-odours of stock and Nicotiana rose up on the vapour of morning's breath and settled on my shoulders, a kiss of favour where the yoke had been. I stood by the window, smoking, and watching the blue exhalation curl, steady, and rush out into the blue air beyond the open window. Here and there in the lawn a blade quivered in the outermost touch of the onshore breeze, flashed in the web of dew, brilliant forgotten stars in the dawn. The stones on the terrace that surrounded the house were dark; the patchy soil in the flower beds was dank and crumby under the dew web, the glossy rhododendron leaves held tight together by it, the sycamores enmeshed. There was no sound from the land; from the garden, from the whole unstructured east, whence the sun came. Where Lyn was.

Adrift in the morning a telephone bell sounded doubly, repeated and repeated and was hushed. An inaudible voice deepened the air with slight vibrations; with life; and after the little ping of the replaced receiver, colours, forms and identities grew in the morning and turned it into day on the wall paper and the Lionel Edwards prints.

Down in the pit of the unwoken house a door squealed and clicked, and the rattle of cups ascended the stair well. Murmurous voices muted by the necessity of balancing tea-trays grew clear and personal on the upper flight. The maids, stylised in black cotton, with white caps and aprons, placed the trays on the table outside my door. O God. How to get back to the bed? Must be in the bed when Doreen comes in. It was unthinkably obvious to be dreaming by the window when the tea arrived. It might be remembered, would give me identity, personality, eccentricity even, when only anonymity was ever safe. I was too ugly, too fat, too desireless for such a romantic pose—would be caricatured by such a pose.

In a frenzy of self-protection I straddled about over the creaking floorboards under the acreage of carpet, shrivelled into the bed, twanging the coiled springs so close under the horsehair mattress with its little pinked leather studs. In a fever I dragged the bedclothes about my ears, tugging at the pillows to surround and hide the high, blue collar of the unsuitable housecoat. In my refuge I could hear them.

'Doreen, will you do downstairs? Please now, for the love of God. Her Ladyship will be rarin' mad by this time.'

'I'll not do downstairs again!' I recognised Doreen's lighter tones. 'You go down. I'll do up here this morning.'

'Much help you are! Go on now, it'd take you no time, and me legs is all swelled up, I'll be hours before I get done.'

'No.'

'Doreen. I'll tell Mr. Grogan on you, and you'll not go down.'

'I'll do her Ladyship, and Mr. Grogan can do the rest. It's more befitting.'

'In what way is that, then? Him blundering about in the Frenchie's room and all that lacy frivolity lying around on the floor. That's not fitting.'

But Doreen was obdurate. I heard the clatter of the tiny silver spoons that had the intricate double lilies worked in miniature upon them. I coveted the spoons, and I coveted the right to engrave lilies where I would.

'Ah, Doreen, for the love of—'

'For the love of me own Christian purity, I'm telling you, Nuala. I'm bringing no more tea in to that Dominic of a morning, if the President himself were to go down on his knees—'

God. Not again. Not AGAIN.

'The Dominic? Doesn't he know? Ah, Mother of God, what's up with the lot of you, these days, I don't know—'

'What's up? What's up? I'll tell you what's up, if you don't know; sticking up in the sheet like Nelson's Pillar, that's what's up!'

Nuala gasped, and the cups tinkled gravely in the wide landing. 'You bold girl. Fancy noticing a thing like that! And passing remark on it! For the love of God—'

'And not for the love of God, either,' went on the irrepressible Doreen. 'Yesterday morning he wasn't there at all, which is no matter, seeing the odd hours he keeps, but ALL HIS TROUSERS WERE. And I know, having done his room this last fortnight, though it hardly looks like a bedroom at all now with all them books in it gathering dust, and all the trouble her Ladyship went to to make it homely for him, with that picture of Our Lady and all.'

I remembered it vaguely, a ravaged girl, with bereaved, bovine eyes in an ivory face. Not very homely. I remembered too a great mass of open books on all the flat surfaces, as if he moved about the room, reading different things as he came to them.

'And furthermore, Nuala, Nora Prosser from Kilmacanogue that's walking out with Willy told him and he told me that she was after him for Confession last week and that he had no tie on. Just that black sweater he wears. So there. At Father Delaney's box and all. And Willy said she said he was in there twenty-three and a half minutes on her watch that Willy gave her. Now what can he ever have done to take that long over? Twenty-three and a half minutes, and he had to borrow the Master's old rosary from her Ladyship, that she's kept since he died, before he went.'

'That's a terrible long time,' Nuala said doubtfully.

'It must be a Reserved Sin to take that long!'

'Get along with you. And that brother of yours ought not to talk about the family so, with you in service here. Most of what he says can be disregarded entirely. But, Doreen, did he come out all right?'

'Of course he came out!' Doreen was scornful of such naïvety. 'It'd take more than Father Delaney to make a mark on that one! But Nora said that the stink of whiskey and perfume in the box after he come out was enough to put an innocent girl out of all ideas of what is godly—'

'For the love of God!—'

'Doreen! Nuala!' Maria's parched voice wailed up the stair well. 'What the hell has happened to my tea? It's after eight, and you gossiping like a pair of midwives.'

'O Lor'. There she goes—' Doreen muttered.

But it was Nuala who answered above the thin trickle of hastily poured tea. 'We was just coming, m'lady. We're in a spot of bother up here.'

'Oh?' Her footsteps slapped on the stone treads. I wondered if she were still wearing the dungarees.

'It's a question of waking his lordship, he doesn't always sleep decent, like,' Nuala explained with simplicity.

'Oh. How tiresome of him. I'll speak to Mr. Grogan about it. But he won't need anything this morning, anyway; he was ill all night. Didn't you hear the goings on up there?'

'No, m'lady. That's a shame. I was saying to Doreen he looked a bit peaky at dinner. Left his soufflé too, and Cook made it special for him, too, seeing that he liked it so much last time.'

'Yes, well. Don't say anything to Cook in case she takes offence. I'll have a word with the Dominic . . . now, for the love of God, will you bring me down my tea!'

As her footsteps pattered down and out of hearing, followed by Doreen's rapid stride, I hid my head in the sheets for shame. The massive dignity of it—'how tiresome of him to upset the maids!'

I thought I had learned a lesson which I would do well not to forget. I thought I had learnt something about being grown up from Maria. I thought that I might learn more about being grown up from Maria than from any one else that I had yet encountered, and that included the Headmistress and the Huntsman of our local hunt. I was ashamed of the patronising opinion I had had of her and knew that I would never forget her rippling forearms swinging the hatchet in the dusty cellar, while her calm voice ranged on and on through the span of

161

experience. I even grew up a little in recognising this and was sobered by my achievement.

After Nuala brought my tea, I got up and prowled around the room with the cup in my hand. All the blackbirds in County Dublin and County Wicklow were gathered in the garden for Lauds. Out on the bog the bog-cotton had dried and lay on the slopes like unseasonal frost, a mirror-life in nature, white where the sun touched it, grey and invisible in the shade. The Sugar Loaf raised its formal shape to the east, sunwards of us. Beyond, the sea glittered a little, blue and mauve over the rocks and sand. There were boats on it, all heading eastwards, sunwards.

◻

The sun rose higher. The soil turned back to dust. The last of the dew web had faded out of the shadows. The cat was sleeping on the hot stones of the terrace. Out on the skyline the horses moved slowly among the heather stalks, marking the passage of time rather than distance, so slowly did they cross the shoulder of the hill. I could distinguish the speck that was Laurence on Arras, though I could never have told how I could isolate this one black dot from the other three. I could not at that distance tell the grey of Carracas carrying Peter or even the difference in heights that marked Topsy, once more relegated to Trottomina (but I thought that she and Francis would inevitably be the two dots close to each other). Bill, Harriet and Stephanie had gone in to Dublin. I was mildly curious to know what sights Stephanie would select to show to the English visitors and how they would differ from those she would have selected had Dominic been of the party. His curtains were still drawn across, fluting slightly in the open window. It was very still on the lawn. I turned idly through the pages of a large book on the post-impressionist French painters, rather vaguely looking for Rousseau. I had found it in the library. I had also glanced curiously at Dominic's table, looking for a packet of cigarettes to steal. I found some among the debris of dead matches, theatre programmes, biro tops and, curiously, a single silk sock, which overlaid the maps and lists. I wondered where its fellow might be. On the blotter he had written, in faint pencil,

'My body is made carrion for my sins
And my soul dispersed about unkindly.
I am nothing more cleverly defined than the
flapping space between the edges of a roughly
broken string
Sweet Mary, give me back my personal
madnesses.'

And near the top of a crumpled sheet of crested writing paper yesterday's date and the words:

'My dear God;
Your manners leave much to be desired.
Don't be so rough with me.'

◘

I had put the writing paper in the waste paper basket, torn up, and scribbled out the lines on the blotter. It was the only thing I ever did for him. I took my book and came out on to the mossy, scentless lawn, stepping over the cat as I came.

It was one of those mornings that more properly belong to Victorian reminiscences than to reality. The sun was very high and the sky quite cloudless. The sycamores drooped above their own shadow, as if they wished to creep down into the heavy cool there. We were sitting on the lawn to the west of the house, below the terrace which at this point ran round the corner of the big drawing room and the side of the dining room and at the end of the house dropped down three steps to the west gate of the little walled-in rose garden. A massive, contorted wisteria covered the granite wall so that the little arch where the gate was almost doubled its width under the pendulous foliage. Behind us the shrubbery gave way to wood, and I wished I could see it in spring, with the bluebells, carnal and abandoned, behind the caustic colours of the punctilious beds. Now the wood was dark and musty, and only the inside leaves closest to the trunks could really be seen as green. It cast no shade on the lawn at this time of day, although it prematurely darkened it in the evenings, bringing memories of odours and dangers whose significance had long been outlived. I liked its strength behind my back. I liked it as a bulwark between the habitation of men and the bog outside, keeping the bog untroubled in its ancient businesses, while the coralled creatures grew acute and mannered in their defined place. So strong and secure was this sense of enclosure that I suffered a feeling of profound unease at the thought of Laurence out there among the other species. It was as if, being removed from ritual and formal time, she were projected into a feral state where all relationships were ambiguous and all states at the limit of their range, so that the slightest fluctuation of intended thought, of memory or of carnal sensation could destroy her or reduce her into the inconsequent growth of the bog flora. I laid down the

164

disputatious brilliance of the pages on Dufy and folded my hands in my lap, willing all things not dead to become instantly inanimate until she return in safety from Outside There.

I was loosely conscious of the incongruity of Grogan in the fresh air before I realised the full impact of his presence on the lawn. I had not yet seen Grogan outside the house, and while I had become indifferent to his soft attentions in the drawing rooms and library and to his covert watchfulness from behind Dominic's massive chair in the diningroom, where he had recently taken up his significant station (thereby causing Maria and Anna evident surprise and some dismay), it had never occurred to me that he might also be seen, as it were, in the wild state. Not that there was anything particularly wild about him at the moment as, clothed in servile black, he issued from the terrace, pausing fractionally on the lower step to glance with distaste at the tall delphiniums which overtopped the terrace wall and flanked the steps, making a cloudy screen against the grey stone, such as my great-aunts and no doubt yours would have found suitable to render in water colours. With gavotte-like movements, Mr. Grogan toe-heeled between the alyssum and the aubretia, the great silver tray carried high above elbow level on the expertly spread palm and fingers, high above rose-bush level, left hand slightly extended to balance, to offset, cuff discreetly gleaming in the sun, eyes lofty above the clinging moss. With one movement Anna, Matthew and I laid down our books and stared at him. He swivelled the garden table into a central position by extending one toe and exposing his suspenders to my disbelieving gaze, but not a drop spilled from the curved spout.

'His lordship suggested that since the weather was so extreme—thank you, miss, sir.'

His withdrawal was an enchantment.

It was the only time that summer that I heard Anna giggle.

There were five cups on the coffee tray, and it was only a minute before we heard a thunder in the undergrowth, a heavy breathing, snappings, swishings in the saplings and Maria's voice like a traveller in an antique land, 'For the love of God! Who had that bright idea?' She emerged on to the lawn, a dryadic nightmare of colourless leaves, dry twigs, dust, her flowered cotton dress worn as a shirt but escaping from the corduroys in the hinder regions, bearing a shears and with a scout knife maliciously poking from her pocket. 'I was just thinking that I felt a little need for something, but I didn't think of coffee on the lawn.'

Politely we nodded to indicate that we did indeed sympathise with her former idea but were even more delighted by this manifestation, spectacular and unusual though it was. Abandoning herself in Matthew's proffered chair she poured the coffee out, managing to give the impression that she knew she was doing something just a little naughty.

'The change in Grogan since that boy arrived! He must have gone out and bought a hundredweight of pep pills, or whatever the things are, and a dozen new shirts when he heard who was coming. And all because the boy offered to bring his own servant to help out with this week. Very civil of him, I thought, but Grogan was wild.'

'Jealous?'

'Jealous and proud, Matthew my pet. Silly man, God help him if he relapses into his old ways now that I know what he can do. Still, it's natural enough, a man is a man, which is more than a woman ever is.'

With this obscure pronouncement she relapsed against the pyjama-striped canvas, sipping noisily and blowing on her cup. A little scatter of raw, dead vegetation settled around her on the green. She might have been there for a millennium, contributing a steady increase to the humus horizon, so intimately involved did she appear in her garden setting. Near her, nightmare Anna sat as still as a delicate decoration, Matthew sprawled at her feet, her golden hair tinting the worked intricacies on the massive silver service where the raised patterns reflected the superior colour in the sun. More work for our great-aunts.

I was trying tactfully but sternly to indicate to Maria the fact that Daddy had been a landscape gardener and not a latter-day Mr. McGregor ('Never did think Monica was inclined to a vegetative existence—often wondered about that. Do tell me, was he nice?') when Dominic appeared on the terrace. Instantaneously Grogan, who must have been lurking in the wisteria, ventured another progress across the sward, this time bearing a deck-chair. He ignored Maria's cynical grin, erected it with precision, felt the coffee pot, and retired with it for replenishing. Maria snorted. Grogan's back just perceptibly weakened under the load of her scorn, but he stayed true to his purpose and achieved the garden gate without haste. Dominic, who must have fully appreciated the comedy staged for his benefit, gave no sign of having observed it and settled himself into the new chair with supreme assurance. He murmured a general greeting and imme-diately retired behind a pair of impenetrable sun-glasses.

Maria glanced at him, I thought uncertainly. 'I expect you would rather have brandy,' she offered.

Horrifyingly, he blushed.

Immediately Maria blushed, and I blushed.

Into the stricken, crimson moment Matthew said, 'With you on the scene he'll probably produce iced Beaujolais, and your efforts to get extra-curricular coffee will be shattered by his goodwill.'

Dominic smiled, and the enormity subsided, swallowed into the pale ether.

'I hope you don't think it presumptuous of me, Maria, but it was an idyllic concept,' he said softly. 'And I go for coffee much as Gerald went for harder stuff. I am that much of a smaller man than he was.'

'Good God! Talking about conception, boy,' Maria spun round to glare at him, her face contorted and impatient.

'Were we?'

'No, yes, but did Grogan tell you?'

'He didn't tell me anything about conception. I know about that. From Gerald, you know—'

'Dominic, don't be frivolous. This is serious.'

I suddenly knew what 'bated breath' meant. I was bating mine. WHO? with WHOM? O God—But he was anxious all the same.

'Well, tell me.'

'There was a telegram at half seven this morning. From your cousin. He's had a son.'

'William? It's early.'

'Yes. But the message says it's healthy and doing well. Grogan took it; it's on the hall table for you.'

'What does it say, exactly?' He looked so strangely touched, concerned.

'It says, ''Baby born last night. Crispin Dominic Marie. He and Alys well. Regards William.'' Or more or less that.'

'Crispin Dominic; are you sure ab out the Dominic?'
'Quite sure.'
They looked at each other and looked and looked. Nightmare Anna sat very still, her foot against Matthew's arm. Eventually Dominic said, 'Oh well. Thank God,' very slowly and clearly. Then again, 'Thank God,' and in the quiet garden he began to laugh like a man coming out into the coloured world beyond jail gates after a long time there. 'He would never see how tactless that is,' he said, 'but he is gloriously realistic.'

I thought that the glint in Maria's eyes was not from merriment, but it may not have been tears; may not.

Seeing Matthew's and my bewildered faces he said, 'Traditionally the senior males in our family are called Dominic. William is my heir. It is just that he has made it very clear by this that he doesn't expect a long future for me.'

'And you are amused?' Matthew said brutally.

'Yes. Wouldn't you be? He's perfectly right to do it. I rather admire him. Or I would if I didn't know him.'

They smiled at each other across the sunlight with a tenderness that made the day gaudy among the bright flowers, and Matthew reached out his hand and touched Dominic's sandalled foot with a quick, sure gesture. Embarrassed, I looked away, and Dominic went on smiling. When the coffee came he sent Grogan back into the house for glasses, ice and champagne. The sun rose even higher and even hotter. There were no horses in sight, and slow emotions drifted through the heat. By the time the riders had returned the champagne was on the table, rugs scattered on the grass, and something of a human colour was tinging Dominic's grave face.

It was the supreme achievement of nature that the sun was in its zenith as she came through the iron gate to

drink iced champagne on the lawns. He had climbed and
climbed, striving with angelic wit to reach heights
beyond appreciation, and now stood, outside universes,
upon the pinnacle of time. She came slowly, her hair,
her eyes, her smile, geysers of reserved light. Her step
emboldened the dark grass into brilliance. Her motion
succeeded that of the sun, who now began to come down,
carefully, to the lure of her progress. Far away, very far
away the pale delphinium bells began to ring, ding
dong, ding dong, d—

'Laurence, we're waiting for you,' Dominic called.
He had a clear light voice that cut across the bells. 'We
are celebrating. I am provided with heirs unlimited, but
much more significant, Maria is a great-aunt! Alys had a
son last night, and the church bells will be rung in his
honour, or someone's honour, at five this evening. The
interim we will fill in a suitable manner, such as toasting
Maria in champagne. Take a glass, here, and give me a
kiss, and you can talk French for the rest of the day to
celebrate, and Maria is allowed to blaspheme, and I to
talk rubbish and stutter as much as I like, and anyone
can be rude to anyone else with impunity. Pop. There
she goes—Christ, nearly got the cat, sorry, catty;
Matthew, pass them round. Did you see the Dublin lot
on your way in?'

'I thought I heard a car,' Francis told him.

Suddenly Laurence said, 'Sin of omission.' She was
standing close to me. She had a blade of coarse grass in
her left hand and was running her right thumbnail up it,
so that it was shredded out into a fan of miniature grasses.
They were very sharp. I could see the muscles in her
back move under the creamy shirt as she spoke. Her
legs long and straight in the boots and breeches made

her almost as tall as Dominic. Her hands were nervous and brown on the shredded grass blade, the nails narrow and filbert. The bony ballerina's head was bent. I could smell faintly the lavender smell of her in the garden airs.

'And omission of sins, my dear,' he murmured, watching her flicker at the endearment.

'You have not mentioned that I too am a great-aunt.'

'You can't be!' Peter said, laughing at the absurdity of Laurence being a great-aunt. 'You're far too young.'

'I am Maria's half-sister, therefore I am a half great-aunt.'

'I wondered who you were,' Topsy said casually.

I fought down a blistering temptation to strike her into the mossy grass. As if we hadn't all wondered who the hell she was, who had never been explained, never quite counted in, never quite ignored. Topsy's remark made her anonymity a mountain of obscurity in our minds. It had never occurred to me, and I am sure to the others, to wonder so subtly just why we did not know who she was, until Topsy made it crassly obvious with a champagne glass in her hand.

'My mother—' she began, her long eyes narrow in the thin, chestnut skin of the lids.

'Neither your mother nor mine is relevant to this child. Their connection with him, since it does not appear as if either you or I will have daughters for him to marry, is a purely formal, not to say retrospective, one.'

So he knew, did he? Or was it blind ignorance? Was I becoming obsessed, unable to see anything in its own light, but all things only ever in mine? But I thought, 'he knows'.

'Hey,' Peter said, suddenly, 'That's rather pessimistic.'

'Say I'm rude and be honest. But I'm not being rude.

171

Do you intend to bear daughters, Laurence?'

She looked slantwise at him. 'I'd drown them like kittens.'

Peter glared at her. Offer gallantry and see what happens, his tight mouth said. He wriggled inside his waistband and shrugged. Dominic watched him and laughed. I was aware of an animosity I had not noticed before. If they had not been talking across Laurence I might have been amused; as it was I endured the ice of her exclusion like an insult.

But Dominic said, 'Laurence and I, my dear, ignorant fellow, share a knowledge of the female of the species which you will never know. For this reason we would drown our daughters and refuse your chivalry. Right, cousin?'

'Right, Dominic. But you are more vulnerable than I.'

'Very true. Peter, I will not turn my fists on you till you give me the excuse. But take care when you do. I have long arms.'

'Don't be childish, Dominic. Anyway I wouldn't fight you.' Peter looked like an enveloped hedgehog, all prickly and round, with, one knew, a sweet little pink nose in there somewhere.

'Yes, Dominic, you are being childish,' Maria said suddenly. 'No one wants to know about either of you, and anyway no one knows what you are talking about, so carry on your back-biting somewhere else or be quiet.'

In reply Dominic put his left arm around Laurence's shoulder, and to my terror I saw her slide hers around his waist. My mouth went dry as I watched the two browned arms, so alike, so thin, with ligaments and muscles twanging like stricken wire about the two tall frames as, Dominic whistling between his teeth, they began the sort of stooping, stepping, ducking ritual that precedes the mating of the bigger birds. (Or it might have been a dance that precedes the violence of the cock birds' fight.) Mesmerised we watched, I in a frenzy, Maria coarsely amused, Matthew with a great, and it seemed misplaced, pity in his ugly face.

Topsy said, 'Don't they look silly.'

'No,' Francis said, and his eyes were wide and hunted.

Still Dominic whistled, a high insistent little calling over the grass. Bob and sideways, bow and stoop, outside arms like trailing wing tips beyond the stilted hips; it was utterly obscene and very lovely in the sun.

Nightmare Anna said, looking at me (why me?)—'I think they are lovely, Helen.'

I could not reply as they turned slowly about and about and about, but only shook my head. Peter said, 'Honestly!' and turned away, disgust shutting his lips in unwonted severity. The pale champagne glittered in the glasses.

With passionate relief I saw Harriet, Bill and Stephanie emerge through the walled garden. They stopped a moment to watch, and I heard Bill's laughter across the electric air. Dominic looked up, flung his hair out of his eyes and dropped away from Laurence like a stone. She straightened automatically, looking across the lawn. Dominic laughed and shoved the sunglasses right against his eyes. From this hidden position he turned to her, 'I have so many regrets—' he began, in French.

She gave him her hand, holding his fingers very delicately in her palm. 'I have none.'

'Then mine fall away, I suppose. Yes, I suppose so.' She must have been able to see his eyes, they were very close together, for hers dropped.

'Good,' she said brusquely. She did not brush against him as she passed and returned to her chair. I could not keep my reddened eyes from her. Her smile for me was polite and secret, in a foreign tongue. Her flesh was the colour of honey, her eyes as deep as the wings of the Scotch Argus and as velvety, pinned out, fluttering, beneath her brows.

Bill asked, 'What on earth's going on?'

Harriet said, 'Laurie, we bought you a present.'

Stephanie was cut off from him, Peter standing in her path, so that she was forced to look at him, acknowledge him, pass around him on her way to the slight, transient figure in the centre of the group.

Anna said, 'We were watching an exorcism,' and Dominic spun round to her, his eyes black squares of reflection in his estranged face.

Blandly Maria shuffled the flowered cotton around her waist and said, 'I'm a great-aunt, as of twelve hours, and my family find this a source of merriment.' She explained that technically we were celebrating. Bill looked amused, Harriet doubtful.

Dominic gave them champagne and, standing in the middle of us all, raised his glass slowly. We were drawn to our feet, as if he had lifted physically each one of us. Expectantly we awaited the toast. But he said nothing. Very slowly and with tremendous precision he raised his glass, held it out and made the shape of the cross in the air with it. Then he said, 'Crispin Dominic Marie . . .' into the white heat of the mid-day sun.

Anna's face was that of a communicant; *Kyrie, kyrie, kyrie* in the sun . . . The present Dominic took her hand in his and raised it to his lips.

'Crispin mutter mutter' we all went, embarrassed,

and drank the iced champagne, and did not look at her nor him as the circle dissolved, reshaped and spun in the bright colours of the dresses and shirts and the wooing responses of pigeons, and the signals passed from eye to eye and body to body over the little curt grass blades where the mower had been, and Dominic went off, up to the terrace, carrying an unopened bottle, caressing the foil in his overlong fingers, and five minutes later the stable bell started to peal, *Kyrie, Kyrie, Kyrie* across the air and into the blue delphinium bells, swaying in the song, *Kyrie, Kyrie, Kyrie* and from the wide bog beyond the echo, *eleison, son, son,* among the heather bells and the heath bells; *eleison, son, son.*

I sat beside her on the balustrade of the terrace. Cold salmon pinked the green lettucy platefuls. Egg yolks, beetroot and the cream of mayonnaise lustrous in the sun. There was no shade now. I could hear the crisp stalks scrunched between her teeth. I could see the saliva on her lips, clear and sweet on the pink flesh, and I thought of the taste of someone else's saliva, which was a taste I had never tasted. I thought I would like to, fairly immediately. I let my knee rest against hers and thought that there were other things I would like as well. I watched Stephanie resting her knee against Dominic's and grinned through the Russian salad at her. She looked away frostily but ill-advisedly because she turned straight to Peter who grinned too, and between us she had no alternative except a central position which brought her face to face with Maria who was not at her most lovely with a piece of shredded cos between her teeth, twitching and jerking on her chin to the internal rhythm which was subjugating its fellows. I wondered what success Peter thought he was going to have against that sort of competition. She swopped her empty plate for Dominic's full one and began all over again. Dominic watched her placidly. He seemed to derive some internal nourishment from her greed, as if her double share were not double but passed on to him in the mere pleasure of her eating. Harriet and Bill had brought him a penny whistle from Capel Street market, and he was holding it in his right hand, the long, ill-proportioned fingers caressing it gently, like a breast or a piece of velvet. Inside the windows the tall portraits looked out on the terrace, looked out at us eating in the sun. Long, fastidious, eighteenth-century faces watching from behind the glass. Each of them more or less Dominic, from each frame a little of Dominic looking out; and he on the terrace, dark behind the sunglasses, looking out into the sun, too. I wondered when Dominic SanFé would deign to die, and whether the family tomb had a wrought iron grille over it, intricate, in the Spanish manner. As the Thing which separated him from us was worn already; intricate, exquisite, final.

'You find it oppressive?' she murmured. I looked, caught in an instant of macabre desire.

'Very.'

'When HE is dead, I will have money and no purpose other than to buy a sky-blue houseboat. We will buy it on the Garonne and sail up and down past the chapels and the unfenced fields, and we will buy new bread and old wine and thin sliced sausage, and eat in thunderstorms between the vineyards. Sausage and cheese and milk in the lightning, and great bites from whole loaves in the thunder. Will we? And never, ever forget that Monday is early closing?'

We stared at each other across the balanced plates.

'Again?' I asked.

'Yes, again.'

'Yes. I don't mind. I would not mind that.'

She dropped her face into her hands and I looked away, wondering with whom she had had that picnic and hoping that I would never know.

And so I too was implicated. I had no money to buy a sky-blue houseboat.

Letter xlviii

My love;

I cannot put this in the story book, because I do not know how to tell it. I have no memory of what went before, or of what happened at the time, except to me and to him. You will have guessed, of course, and anyone else, otherwise why bother with the story. But I had not guessed. I was totally innocent of malice, and of malice as represented in the world. There is no one to accuse, no one to punish, no one to weep with. It was just one of those things.

We were sitting on this terrace, you see, in the sun. I was thinking about the sky-blue houseboat. Someone, Topsy, or Stephanie even, I don't know, made some remark which provoked Bill to enquire how the hell she had been educated. Some mistaken fact or name, I don't know. I was vaguely aware of the voices. Maria asked me, I don't know why, where I was at school. Stephanie said, Ashbury Hall. I wasn't really listening.

I only remember his face, suddenly coming through the sunlight, and his voice, saying over and over again, 'Ashbury? Near Swindon? That Ashbury? The one near Swindon? That one?' until he reached me, and I could not see through his dark glasses. Because by then I did know.

I said, 'Yes. That one.'

He must have gone down on his knees then, on the stones, because he held my upper arms in his hands, and I was looking slightly down at him, when he said, 'And the girl, the girl in Upavon. Helen, tell me her name.'

So I told him her name, in full, very clearly, very carefully, so that there might never be any misunderstanding between us.

He said, 'Yes. Yes,' and then he got up, and he walked away from the terrace and out across the lawn, and disappeared from our sight.

And after a little while I got up and walked into the house, and it was dark in there and smelled of lavender, wax and turf and some summer flower.

It was just one of those things; and so here I am.

When you have read all this, we will take out my letters to you and change the names and the places and the dates, and a few other intimate details, and we will hawk it off in a brown paper parcel round the publishers of romantic fiction. And when they turn it down, I'll bet you five double whiskeys that the stated reason will be, 'It's unskilful; life's not like that.'

It's just one of those things; life is like that, unskilful, hey?

Helen

◉

What are these three lily stalks doing in my room; and all this snow? The flowers must be up there somewhere —beyond the grave lid, the other side of the clouds.

178

Maybe one day I will climb through the iron pattern and up the stalks and find the flowers. You can sit in them, on the water. Jeremy Fisher did. How close together they are—I can only just get through, fighting the cold lemon sunlight for a passage. The beads of condensation on the stalks are cold on my forehead, sticky on my hands. I lift my hand to my face and see faces reflected in the little drop. Other Face. The other drops are falling on the linen, making a ticking noise. They have faces in them too, but I do not look at these because they are falling from the Spanish grille above the grave, and I am afraid they will have made the sheet wet. I cannot tell whether that crackling noise is from the icicles in the sheet, formed of the face-drops, or my ribs because they have wound me so tight in the linen. I would like some lilies, but they would not show under all the snow. Snow is very heavy, it presses me down, and I would like to go further down, right into the rock, out there beyond where the curraghs came, or the herring, and before. If I give it time to settle; but it takes so long to filter through the grille. When I turn my head this way I can see one of the faces quite clearly. It has melted around the lips, which are quite wet and of a curious blue colour. The cold, I suppose. I am very afraid it is going to speak.

'Hello, hello,' it says. It can't be a spirit, they talk in archaisms. Certainly they don't say hello, hello.

I do my party trick for it and say, 'Hi!'

It says, 'Is that Helen Wykham?'

I am reserved and say cautiously, 'It might be; or someone else.'

It is very friendly and has a familiar shape to the nostrils. 'Well, hello,' it says, 'This is Helen Wykham here. I have news for you. She was only a girl, like any other.'

'Not like any other.'

'Oh yes. Exactly like all the others he has been with. I know, I've seen him at it. There is a keyhole in your door, you ought to have a peep one day. He does pretty things with them when he gets—'

'Not with her,' I interrupt, shouting.

'Think not? Remember those wide flat hips, Helen? And he loves long legs—she had lovely long legs, hadn't she? Hadn't she, Helen?'

'Shut up. I am not listening to you—' I shout again. Help help, I am not listening.

'Where do you think they did it? Up on the downs above Upavon? You know that place where you and I had that picnic one day, that was all screened in with bushes?'

'No, no no not there. I have been there, no no no—'

'One of those afternoons, the Friday or Saturday of half-term, maybe. He likes to do it in the light, so he can watch . . .'

'Not look at her, not her, those parts—no NO. Jesu, GO AWAY.'

'Do you think she looked too, or were her eyes screwed tight against the sight of that face, or that—'

'SHUT UP. O God, have mercy—'

'Or even against the sun, warm on her cheeks, because he was doing it that way where the woman lies on her back and opens her legs, and the man—oh, don't make such a fuss!'

'I will kill you. Kill you,' I whisper, but cannot turn my head in case I see, there.

'Don't be silly, you can't kill ME!'

'O Jesus.'

'O Adonai! The soft outer bit, and then all those wet little red intricacies of flesh, and the timothy grass on either side, and between even, and the discarded briefs in the shade there on the left, and the larks' song above that little noise—'

'I cannot hear you. You may talk on, and I simply cannot hear—'

'You can't help hearing. Turn your head, Helen and see who is talking.'

I have turned my head, now.

MIRROR, MIRROR ON THE WALL

Hung at a slightly tipping angle so that I can see the thing that really matters, darling, would you mind, just a little further, yes, that's almost exactly right; would you be satisfied with that, madam, it is so hard to guess at heights without being, ha, ha, unduly intimate, and the customers tend to resent that; thank you, darling, that will be all for today, thank you, madam,

WHO IS FAIREST OF US ALL

What are these three lily stalks doing, swaying in my room, and all this snow?

I didn't consider it stealing this time. I just walked into his room and took a whole packet from the top of the chest of drawers. The bottle of brandy was there as well, with a mouthful left in the bottom. I drank it, gratified to find that it was more like a glassful, and left the top off and the bottle lying on its side. A thought struck me and I opened the top drawer. His wallet was there, and I rifled it carefully. It was a curiously impersonal receptacle and held nothing of value to me. Except the money. There were no photographs of her, indeed none at all; no personal letters, nothing to suggest her. I knew men carried more than money in their wallets. If she had been more than Helen Wykham had just said she was, there would have been something . . . a letter, an old theatre ticket, something. There was nothing at all. Just money. Enough to buy a sky-blue houseboat. Each note was folded over carefully, symmetrically, so that he would never hand out two for one, or a fiver for a single. I liked the cold, pale look of it; I liked all that spending-power, couchant, crude, in the initialled wallet. I liked his initials; L.D.M.S. You couldn't make words out of it. I liked his hair brushes, too, but they had G.D.M.S. on them. I still liked his cufflinks with two lilies on them; and I hated him.

I didn't take any of his money, it would have been stealing.

I went back upstairs to my room and opened the packet of cigarettes. There was too much between us now for me to consider it as anything other than trivial to walk into his room and take a packet. He was the only person in the house who would be certain to have some to spare. I washed the blood off my forehead; it must have got there when I banged my face on the bedside table. It came off easily enough. I wandered off to the bathroom, ascended the dais and sat on the mahogany bench, piddling merrily on the hand-painted garlands of briar roses in the bowl. On my way back I went in to Stephanie's room and cast about in there, emerging with the vast plastic holdall she used to transport her cosmetics. I had thought of a motto. It was, 'If you can't beat 'em, join 'em.' I thought Francis might tell me what it was in medieval Latin. I was taking timothy grass as my device and thought that I would put a bar sinister across it, and then reflected that that was rather rude to Mother.

I rifled Stephanie's mysteries, taking the razor to shave my armpits, a thing I had never done before, being so suffused with shame by them that I could not bring myself to do anything about them other than cover them up; I took the cream that takes hairs off your chin, the emery paper for whittling down the ones on my legs, and the shampoo. I left the contraceptive jelly and the false eyelashes as being unlikely to be needed in a locked bathroom. I also found Daddy's signet ring. It fitted the third finger of my right hand, and I have not taken it off since.

In the bathroom I took the mirror off its hook, laid it out on the floor and squatted over it, examining myself minutely. I thought what I saw was rather coarse but physiographically identical with the illustrations in the medical books on the quays, 20p a volume. Satisfied, I replaced the mirror and washed scrupulously, even my hair, dried myself 'with great attention to all cracks and creases and intimate places' and feeling decidedly depilatoried, lay on my bed while my hair dried. I read the remainder of *Why Didn't They Ask Evans?* which I had filched from the bathroom in Enniskerry, decided that I wouldn't have asked her either, wrote carefully in the fly leaf—'Enniskerry; dawn dances; *post vomitarium*. SanFé L.D.M. *inter alia*; Aug.'—and began to dress.

I spent twenty minutes turning up the hem of my dress, sewing my finger to the linen on three separate occasions, and listening to Dominic moving down below in his bedroom. On my way downstairs I took three big carnations of suitable hue from a bowl on the first floor landing table and stuck them low on my hip with a safety pin taken from my sister's blue bra strap, which I had found on returning her cosmetics with a note scrawled in her lipstick that said, 'took some, left others, good luck, Ta. H.' I knew she would be cross, and that she would understand the cryptic message. I was looking forward to a dash of that dry sherry. It was ten past seven. After five and a half hours not even my sister had thought of looking for me.

For some frivolous reason it had been ordained that we should consummate the house-party by an evening in the local drinking establishment where, it transpired, Maria was surprisingly wont to go after Confession on a Friday evening. She declined to join us, despite Dominic's urging, and I was disappointed. The idea of Maria leaning on the bar, downing Irish among her tenants, had been alluring, but she must have felt that Dominic's presence would threaten her insouciance in some way, so she refused. She and Laurence went to Confession together in one car, Beauty and the Beast reduced to orthodoxy and rite.

Dominic, Anna and Francis also went; Dominic dangling a worn black rosary against his thigh, running the groups through his fingers monotonously while the little figurine dangled and jiggled on the end of it. I knew that Father Delaney's box was too small to hold him and his sins and the figurine. I wondered which would be rejected. I prayed that the pitiful Francis would not be able to remember him in his prayers. I was new to hatred, not quite organised around it. We had only been companions for seven hours or so at that time.

There is a calm acceptance of the viciousness of man which governs the interior decoration of the Irish Bar. I found it an acceptable setting in which to come to know my new companion. Matthew brought us—Protestants with no Confessor to distract us from our selected paths to hell. I had been to one or two of those English pubs where they hang horse brasses on the walls and serve shandy after church on Sundays, but these licentious incursions into the realms of Serious Drinking (as opposed to Social Drinking, which I had a vocation for, and which in any case it was my duty to enjoy) had always been in the company of someone's father, and there is nothing less conducive to a serious approach to bibulosity than 'my Dad' offering you ginger ale. Into an Irish Bar I had most emphatically never ventured, my wildest moment to date having been in Dominic's company when we drank in the private bar of a very exclusive semi-eating house before the abortive visit to the theatre. I think we were all a little daunted by the inhospitable door, the plastic varnish, the lavatory glass with Guinness inset in frosted emblems across the windows. Even Matthew, accustomed to the unimaginable viciousnesses of Bray, or worse still, Amiens Street after dark, hesitated fractionally before thrusting the door open. It hissed like a clutch of young serpents as we passed through.

Inside, hanging on the wall above the fireplace immediately below the two shields which carried the arms of the two houses which stand on either side of the valley where the village is, hung a coloured calendar. I don't suppose that I would even notice it now. That night it appalled me. It supported a female in what appeared to me to be the briefest suggestion of clothing that could be made public, with a glass in one hand and her left breast in the other. She had a weird, wide smile and false teeth. She was in full colour. I cannot remember if it was the idiocy of the unerotic smile or the violence of the luscious flesh that upset me so, but I do remember that her upturned, cardboard gaze was directed almost exactly at the great SanFé lilies above her.

Matthew led us to the window seat where an unfrocked pew, two piano stools and one of the benches that the second eleven sit on while they wait to go in to bat did duty as an irregularly tempered window-seat. All around the wall, pressed against the walls, the people of the parish disposed themselves upon similarly vicariously assembled furnishings. In total silence they exuded a strong odour of old incense (this being a ritual post-confessional levity), milk, Outdoors, cow, and other more hominid ingredients. Terrified, I looked away. Pale, damp eyes regarded us, without animosity, without welcome. Stephanie sat down on the pew, carefully crossing her legs. They all stared at her knees. Harriet sat beside her, tugging at her skirt. They all stared at Harriet's knees. Topsy swizzled in on her bottom, jostling them along a fraction. They all stared at Topsy's knees. I leant over the back of the pew.

'Well, um, what'll we have? Gin?' Peter said, but it came out in a hoarse whisper. He cleared his throat and started again, louder. The Eyes watched him.

'Yes, please. Strong,' Stephanie said in a high voice. I started to giggle. 'Shut up!' she hissed.

I suffered a tremendous urge to take my knickers off, or start in on the Agincourt speech, or pretend to be a beaver, and clung to the pew-back to prevent my body inadvertently commencing any such activity.

Stephanie moaned, 'You beast, you beast.' I looked quickly around, incensed that any one should take advantage of her natural reticence in such surroundings. 'O, you brute, give over, oh, fuck OFF,' she whispered, *in extremis*.

I could see nothing untoward. I straightened my back, glared, clenched my fists on the pew-back, to no avail. She moaned again. Horrified I stooped over her. 'Stephanie, Stephanie, what's wrong?'

As I moved she let out a little squeal. The bartender dropped a tin ashtray. Peter and Matthew made uninformed sudden gestures: the Eyes hardened: I had my hand on her hair, pulling it agonisingly over the pew back. Muttering abasing apologies I sat on a piano stool. I recollected how that very evening I had turned my skirt up two and a half inches, sewing my fingers to the hem three times. I accepted a gin and Italian, a drink I abhor. Since I had removed the friendly fuzz from under my arms I now experienced the novel and alarming sensation of individual sweat drops trickling straight down into the wrinkle under the arm of my bra. I wondered how extensive it would prove as a reservoir and how many drinks would be needed before the drops tickled unbearably as they passed down my ribs in a tiny Poulaphouca of despair.

It was their hair; that eruption of gold, amber and worn bronze, dancing and flickering about their heads. They all moved very fast and certainly, relieved of the enormities of their souls, perfumed, rare, slight in the bare bar. Dominic's voice was raised in collective greeting, eliciting a scattered response from the Eyes; I heard the loud sounds of him pulling another table over, dragging chairs, unaware, unresponsive to our uneasiness. He hustled us into a round of more cheering drinks; he made sublime, confident excursions to the bar and back, his stammering voice clear above the clink of glass and money. He moved us about, a circus of dumb creatures, so that he could sit beside my sister, and so that Bill had room with Harriet. He lit cigarettes, he talked, he twisted his fingers in and out of Stephanie's abused hair, he brushed the dust of Father Delaney's box off the knees of his white trousers, he removed his tie, he settled down to drink. It was a perfectly contrived performance. I missed none of it. Nor did the Eyes. I thought I would get him soon enough.

'Who is that?' I asked Anna suddenly.

I had been vaguely aware of a man leaning against the lid of the varnished upright piano that stood opposite the fireplace. Like the rest of the men in the bar (and they were mostly men) he had pale eyes. But his were different in that they were cold and yet in some way violent. He had been staring at Dominic for some time, and every now and again he passed a damp tongue quickly over his lips. He put me in mind of a ferret one of my cousins had once kept. The ferret had had nasty ways with rabbits and had eventually been throttled by the gardener's wife with a piece of wire after the celebrations on Easter Sunday.

Anna looked at me blankly. I had noticed that in certain humours she wore very bright colours, and she was now dressed in a flame-coloured shift which emphasised the strange calm of her face and her wide, empty eyes.

'Why, that's Willy Maguire, Doreen's brother from Kilmacanogue,' she said, and smiled. 'Doreen has Friday evenings off, usually, and he comes up here to meet her. I like his face, it's stimulating.' She smiled at me again, and I smiled back, because I had found those evil little eyes stimulating too, and now there were three.

I drank heavily, watching us closing in for the kill. I counted Peter among us; and then we were four. Someone turned the radio on, and a blast of heart beat beating scoured us. Dominic stirred irritably, his eyes flickering around. I saw Willy Maguire note the movement, and his blunt fingers twiddle the knob so that the sound came fractionally louder. I asked, 'Do they ever dance, Anna?' thinking it a monstrous thing in nature that such shapes should become fanciful with their feet.

'Oh, yes. I believe so. I have never been here before. Ma comes.'

I wanted to ask if Maria danced. Solo, presumably.

'I have always wanted to dance with Willy,' she went on. 'You would like to dance with Willy, wouldn't you?'

'I would like to dance with you,' I replied recklessly.

'But I think we are, Helen,' she said enigmatically. 'On the Dominic's grave, perhaps? He is assured of his heirs, now. He has no need to marry, has he? He will buy Mother off. God bless this child. I have been praying for him all day. Crispin Dominic Marie. This Dominic will go away now and leave us all in peace. I want peace.'

'So does Francis.'

'Dominic will deal with Francis. He will know how to; he understands a lot of things. Matthew tells me, and Matthew loves him.'

I looked at Francis. He had his back to the curtains, cheap cotton affairs with luxurious green and purple growths depicted in rectangular frames, so that he looked like a forgotten martyr in the worst period for stained glass. Topsy was trying to get him to put his arm around her, wriggling up and under his shoulder so that he was compelled either to acquiesce or to move away un-chivalrously. Topsy's face was beginning to blur in the gin, as she inched up under his little biceps, and a tiger plant ran amok with orange leaves behind her. I looked longingly at her. It wasn't that I liked her; it was years since I had liked her. I just thought she was terrific with her innocent, hard face and her innocent, hot lust. And brave, playing games with reality like that. I thought her lust more culpable than mine, being so simple and so possible, and so easily achieved. We wrote different kinds of story-books, she and I. Hers would always find the public. Mine most likely never. To be simple seemed then, in the gin and the pop sound, the very ecstasy of bliss. And the little bitch didn't deserve any such ecstasy.

Dominic got up to dance. It was early for dancing. He kicked his shoes off and took Harriet in his arms, pressing his face down on her hair so that they could not see each other's faces. Everybody in the room watched them; no one could see their faces. In any case they had lost them in the heart beat break beat of the radio. Topsy wriggled. Francis gave in, looking as if he were about to cry. The Eyes absorbed it all, turned it into nothing, and returned to the froth on the Guinness glasses. I remembered how Peter and Stephanie used to look when they danced; something a shade different from now; somehow more victorious, less personal. I bowed down over my gin. 'He'll kill her.' I had spoken aloud.

The great hand on my knee was Matthew's. The great eyes drawing me up were Matthew's. They blurred and shivered. 'No,' he said.

I said, 'When Daddy died, we went to his funeral in the church. We didn't go to church much except for the Carols and Christmas Day. That Christmas we went, Mother and Stephanie and me. And she had a white muff and a white furry hat. She was fourteen, and she looked like that.' I was trying to tell him something, but I wasn't sure quite what it was. The music had the same rhythm as *Ding-dong merrily on high* and I tapped my feet to it. I went on, 'Mother put up decorations for it. She wasn't very good with hammer and nails, and she doesn't like heights, but she climbed up to the top of that bloody ladder and beat her thumbs into pulp getting streamers up for us. For Stephanie and me. It was Christmas, you see, and Stephanie looked like that.'

He said, 'Yes. I see,' and I think he truly saw something which I never have, quite. I only saw that Francis was not very steady on his feet.

'Is Francis tight?' I asked.

'Unfortunately, yes. So is Bill, and so are you.'

'*Ding-dong verrily the sky*', I carolled in response, '*In heaven the bells are ringing! Ky - y - y— . . . rie elei - ei - ei - SON,*' like the heather and the heath.

Bill looked up in surprise. 'Come and dance with me,' he yelled across my shouting.

'Hello, ello-ello, hello-ello-ello, hello—' I called, rising at an angle and finding my nose in the tiger plant, like a Dutch doll in a shipwreck. My feet were awfully far away and awfully small when you considered that I weighed ten and three-quarter stone. I rather wished that I had got those shoes with the tiny ankle straps; they wouldn't look silly now my feet were only THAT size . . .

Ooh, he was lovely, he was. I cuddled into him because I knew he wouldn't fall over, and he kept his feet well out of my way, and he didn't spin me round faster than my head was already going, and he sang *Gloria in excelsis* too, and we had a smashing time, and I never even felt his thighs much less anything else and asked him for another some time, saying truthfully that it was the nicest dance I had ever had in my life, which he didn't for a moment believe.

'Look,' he said, 'There's Doreen.'

And there she was, neatly drinking port with her brother, and Dominic gazing at her from the bar where he was leaning in the totally relaxed posture that comes from long habit. I thought he looked as if he slept like that, leaning on a stained bar. Bill turned back for Harriet, and Dominic just leaned and looked and Willy Maguire licked his lips and Doreen Maguire sipped at her port, and someone turned the radio off when Francis tripped and sent the scarlet, tin ashtray clanking and bouncing on the tiled floor. And all the eyes looked from Willy Maguire's flicking tongue to Dominic's sheltered eyes and down to the ashtray, lying like an admission of sins on the repetitive floor. Then Dominic turned away to pay for the drinks, while the bar-man scribbled the sums on a paper napkin, and began a formalised dance of his own, to and from our table, each time carrying two glasses, eight steps there and back, and no one moved to help him, because every time he turned he looked at Doreen Maguire and she looked at him, and we all watched them look. And all the while he was whistling *I was Born under a Wandering Star* between his teeth. And when he slipped in beside Stephanie and stopped the terrible whistling the bar man put the radio on again so that we would forget the sound of it, and Dominic's eyes moved slowly from Stephanie to Harriet to Doreen. And then he looked at me.

'Your crest looks nice, up there,' I said, gesturing at the wall where the idiot whore smiled up at the great double lilies. I had not expected to be able to make him wince, but, as I have said, he was a clever man. 'I've got you,' I thought. 'I've got you.' Amazed at the ease of it, and my own accuracy. Keeping my face blank, I said, 'That's how it was, wasn't it?'

'No.'

'No, no of course not. You're cleverer than that. I wonder how you managed it—'

'Shut up, Helen. Shut up, shut up; you don't know what you are saying.'

I wouldn't take my eyes off him for Matthew. 'I do,' I said, still staring. 'Don't I, Laurie SanFé?'

For some reason the use of his familiar name did it. I thought he was going to kill me, moving like fire around the table, among breaking glass, his hands round my wrists like chains, and my blood leaping in my veins to his, great absences in us both seared and screaming in a terrible unison. I pressed my head against him, and his ribs were like cage bars, iron cage bars. I bit and bit.

'Coward,' I said.

'Don't say it too often.'

We swayed against each other, and someone tried to part us, pulling at my arms and my dress so that I clung to him, and my strength was the purest in the world. I beat at him with my head, and he swayed again, and I could feel the whole length of his body like a white hot sword against me, and every scream in me went straight into one of those ghastly spaces inside him, and I felt it vibrate in there in the nothing inside of him. And that was one of the happiest moments of my life. When we parted the loss of his arms and the cold air where his chest had been were total pain. Love thine enemy, love thine enemy. The purity of hatred is shattering. Blessed are the pure in heart. The day I lose my hatred, I will die. I said, 'The day I stop hating you, I will be dead.'

But he went out, and when I went out to get away from the shocked faces and the shocked silence, I heard him being sick in the elderberry bush behind the car-park, murmuring her name, 'LYN, Lyn, Lyn, Lyn, Lyn . . .' over and over again so that it came out with the vomit into the dark leaves. They were very gentle with me when I went back, which surprised me. Perhaps they were very slightly afraid. I was sober and strong. I was still alive. The night was young. The radio was playing *I was Born under a Wandering Star* to mock him.

They said things like, 'Are you all right?' and 'Have a drink' and 'Don't worry.' So I had lots of drinks. I wasn't worried, why should I worry?

But he came back after a while, and they all wriggled, and the Eyes speculated, and Matthew leaned forward impulsively and touched him, but he shook his head and hadn't the will power or the courage to end the party, when suddenly Francis started to hiccup into the miserable. gin-sodden boredom of it all, and Bill laughed. It was only a quarter past nine.

It got dark soon after that, and they drew the curtains and turned the radio up again. Dominic settled in for the most deliberate bout of drinking I have ever witnessed. He bought himself a bottle of Jameson and collected a row of glasses. These he lined up in front of him and filled each one. Very methodically he started to drink them, going from left to right. Harriet started to cry. Anna folded her hands in her lap and watched minutely, like a cat. Peter grew whiter and whiter and took Stephanie off to dance, a feat of endurance which lasted through tune after tune on the radio. Topsy followed with Francis but came smartly back again, still towing him, as she couldn't keep him anywhere near vertical. Matthew went to sleep or seemed to. Bill crossed his arms, uncrossed them, fidgeted, drummed on the table, danced with me, with Anna, and finally, rather desperately, with the cook from the hotel behind the village. Behind the bar Micky, the barman, looked up at regular intervals to check. Dominic got up suddenly, and everyone moved back slightly, quickly, but he only went to the bar for cigarettes. Micky said, 'Easy go, now Dominic. It's early yet,' as he tossed the bright pack on the bar top.

Dominic grinned, 'If they can chuck me out of Covent bloody Garden, you can chuck me out of here,' he said unexpectedly.

'Easy up, now,' Micky repeated, professionally.

Dominic came back. 'Cheers,' he said, raising his glass to me. We were smiling at each other, in perfect understanding.

Suddenly it was Francis who lost his head and started pounding on the table with his fists. 'Stop it, stop it!' he shouted, standing up and leaning over the table, his face thrust into Dominic's.

Dominic leaned back and considered him. 'I'm not at all sure that I can,' he murmured.

'Stop it, stop it I say. You're revolting, you're lewd. That's what you are—lewd—I'll make you stop!'

'Sit down, Francis, and either drink up or shut up.'

'I won't drink. And nor shall you—you—' he mouthed helplessly and leaned over, grabbing one of the glasses. He flung it to the floor, and a moan of Aahh came from the watching people around the walls. Micky stepped forward, and Francis hurled another glass down. Dominic and Matthew caught him by the arms, Dominic shaking him like a rabbit till he started to go green and Matthew said, 'That's enough.'

They let him go, bigger, bolder than he, and he twisted and wept behind the table, while Topsy dragged at his sleeve and he hit blindly at her consoling hands. 'Christ, you bastard,' he said at last. 'Let me get out of here. Let me go.'

Matthew stood aside for him, and as he passed, Francis swept the remaining glasses from the table and darted for the door. 'Aah, aaah' they moaned as the whiskey trickled into the cracks in the lino, and Dominic leaped to the varnished doorway and held his arms out, so that he blocked Francis, who stood helplessly pushing at him, the tears running down his cheeks, crying, 'Let me out, let me out, oh, PLEASE Dominic, please—'

And Dominic just stood, looking down at him, not moving.

'Laurie, stop it!' It was Harriet. 'Stop tormenting everyone. Let the kid go.'

Dominic said softly, 'Say you love me, Francis.'

'NO. I won't. Get out of my way. Let me go.'

'Say you love me.'

'I won't!'

'Laurie for God's sake—'

Francis reached for his hands as if he would try and pull him from the door. Dominic caught them and stretched them out so that Francis was pinned up to him, like a pale gold Crucifixion against the black shirt. His face was right against those rails of bones, captured against the sharp collar bone, wetting the shoulder with his tears. His child's arms looked pale and broken in the grip of the man.

'Say it. Francis . . .'

I knew he would break, transfixed against all that bitterness, nailed to it by the watching eyes, bone for

196

bone broken against it. He looked up. We could only see the soft, gold hair over his eyes, the tracks down one curved cheek.

'All right,' he whispered, 'I love you. Now let me go.'

He ducked under Dominic's arm and vanished into the street outside. Dumbly Topsy rose and followed him, and Dominic touched Matthew on the shoulder. 'Now go and comfort him,' he said urgently, and Matthew too went out into the dark.

As he faced the Eyes his expression was as blank as a prison wall. The men in the portraits must have looked like that, passing sentence or receiving it.

Now there were five.

Now I understand that I do not need money for a houseboat, and that I have changed my name and can now leave the island. I make some vague gestures in that direction, saying to Stephanie, 'What time does the boat sail?' although I know I have already missed it and must still go back out of this valley where the village is, out on the bog where the clouds are and the cotton grass, to collect her. It is very easy to make boats; schoolboys do it and display them at Earls Court annually. If school boys, then certainly lovers can. I put my hands in my pockets and leaned back, seeing the boat we should build; its intimate cooking equipment; its ropes; the tiny drawers and cupboards; the immaculate narrow cots; hearing the little sounds of our work; the smells we should come to adopt as our own; Jeyes; parmesan, carroway, a particular talc, and tar; the touch of tarpaulin and river mist, of willow leaves in the fingers, and satin ribbons on dancing shoes. I smiled because I had no stockings on, and although I could feel my calves touch each other on the inner sides, it was for the last time ever, and I bore no resentment. It was too late for that, thank God. Still smiling I looked up and met Anna's smile. I put out my hand to touch the purity of her, but she drew back a little, and the radio vowed that the Lord above had made man to help his neighbours and it told how one might be out when the neighbours came to call, and so I said, 'I won't be out, Anna,' and heard my voice and some other sound which might have been a cock crowing, or a clock ticking, or merely dew settling on the ropes, repeated three times. Dear God, it is so late, and I am so very very drunk!

The air grew stale and stank of staleness. Cigarettes were foul in the spilled, fingered marks and dribbles on the table; someone had drawn a face with horns on a beermat, and someone else a game of noughts and crosses. The noughts had won. I yawned widely and immediately drew everyone's attention.

'Come round?' Stephanie asked callously.

I smiled that gentle smile I had acquired from the last third of the gin bottle and nodded. She was leaning up against the piano, her breast protruding against her dress. Peter was beside her, his hand helplessly inactive on the top of the lid, jittering with its private little tokens of desire. Matthew had returned and was standing behind Dominic, kneading his shoulders absently in his big, light hands, his eyes on Anna, dreamy, disturbed, opaque. Bill and Harriet had their heads close together at the bar, a glass between them, shoulders pulled up around them, legs bent, ready; they might have been mourning or plotting or telling dirty stories, it was not possible to say. Dominic was still under Matthew's absent caresses; both hands clutching his groin he was staring at the table, and my toe was against one of his feet. I moved it curiously, but his eyes were wide and unseeing, and he did not move in response, so I sat with my foot against his, in the hallucinatory peace that lies at the roots of hate and of love. Around us, and between us, the hotel cook and the forestry department watchman danced, and the radio gavotted and flirted its sounds across the lino tiles. All the positions were reversed, and real people going about their entertainment, treading past us, unaware of us, uninterested in us, unable to help us; and we sat, or leaned, quietly unable to help ourselves while their voices spoke of real things and real people and real events, and it suddenly dawned on me that we were all missing Topsy.

'What's happened to Francis?' I asked Matthew, blandly.

'He's all right. Or he will be when he's been sick again. I left him telling Maria about his plan to ride in the Grand National against Dominic, and how he would win by jumping Becher's wide, or some such technicality. Maria was very enthusiastic about it and supplied a lot of extra details, peripheral descriptions that Francis' particular fantasy didn't run to. It was rather fun. I wanted to stay and hear the end of it.' His hand meandered in the curls on Dominic's collar, restless, thoughtless.

Dominic looked up, turned to Matthew and said, 'I have a lovely vision of Francis in a black soutane and shovel hat, bareback on a piebald mare, with the cloth all ruckled up about his knees, just ahead of me going around the Canal Corner. I should like to ride at Aintree too. Maybe I will, next spring, though Francis will scarcely have his soutane by then.'

'Would you win?'

'No, no. Nothing exaggerated like that. Anyway Hopkins suffers from agoraphobia and only ever won anything by mistake.'

I said, 'Are all your pictures in black and white?' looking at his clothes.

'Increasing numbers of them are, yes.'

'You're rather nice when you are drunk,' Matthew said and took his hands away, sitting heavily beside him and pouring out a bottle of beer into a dirty glass.

Dominic grimaced at him. 'I'm consistently nice these days, then, but not everyone thinks so.' He took his hands from between his legs and spread them out on the table, running the tips of his fingers up and down the formica top. 'Let's get me drunker and see if it's a cumulative effect.'

He got up and started to move away, but Anna's voice arrested him. 'I want you sober tonight,' she said.

His eyes narrowed, he considered, judged, decided. Matthew sat very still; fear nibbled around my innards. 'I'm far from sober already,' Dominic said.

'But you are not drunk?'

'No. Not really. Somewhat uninhibited, in certain fields, but not drunk. You can always tell when I am drunk, I stop stammering.'

Anna said, 'I like your stammer.'

'I don't.'

I looked at the bulge under his fly and suddenly started to laugh. He raised his eyebrows. I said, 'I have pictures, too. Mine are in colour. I have one of you, making love, with a stammer, like this—' and I gestured with my fore finger, jabbing the air, to and f-fro.

He turned away for the bar, and I sat laughing in the silence he left behind him, until I saw Anna's face, and it stopped me. I drank some more gin and had a little fantasy of my own. On my own. I knew him so well by now, you see. You do see, don't you?

A sudden slam made me jump. My elbow knocked Anna. She coiled up, a little tight spring inadequately controlled. Willy Maguire had flung open the lid of the piano. The dancers turned and stumbled. The Eyes swivelled around the glasses and the cataracts and the cigarette smoke, narrow, inquisitive. Dominic stopped abruptly, half way across the room. Willy and Dominic looked at each other. Somehow, everyone stopped their noise. The barman resignedly turned down the radio yet again. Bill moved out hesitantly from the bar, his hand held out irresolutely to Dominic. Violence. Again. In the tightened muscles, the calculating eyes, the twitching fingers. In Willy and Dominic.

Willy started to move hypnotically across the tiles, one hand trailing behind him, an inarticulate gesture at the piano. Dominic watched, his eyes measuring the distance between them. Little prickles of fear tickled my back and my left eyelid started to twitch.

'Give us a tune, then, Dominic,' Willy said.

Dominic did not answer. He was staring at Willy. And he was frightened. His lips were soft like a child's, his body half turned to the door, his weight poised.

'Come on, give us a tune,' Willy was getting closer.

Dominic didn't move. He had a curious grace, waiting there to run away; the skeletal grace that the creatures have whose only weapon is speed in flight. He was separate, embarrassing, like a whippet or a rare antelope. He was old things and wild things, in a corner. In a corner they turn, at the end, and open their eyes. I was very frightened.

'Play for us, Dominic. Play for us.'

He moved very suddenly. Willy started, his elbows jerking. Dominic turned his back on Willy and continued on his way to the bar. 'A small, single Jameson, Micky, please.'

Whisper whisper, aaah, the noises grew in the thick silence of the dripping measure under the bottle; whisper whisper.

'Dominic—'

'Get me a chair.'

Willy brought a chair and set it carefully in front of the piano. He wiped the seat with his sleeve. Aah, they said appreciatively. Dominic drained the glass, avoided Bill's hand and turned around. 'I'll play for you, on that thing, drunk. Curse you, Willy Maguire, curse you.'

He sat on the chair, his toes feeling the worn places on the pedals, and pressed down the keys, gently, so that no round came; pressing them like switches that would fill the gaps I had felt inside him with something from elsewhere in him. Turning something on in himself.

I was glad he had his back to us. I was glad I could not see his face. I am glad I was too young and too ignorant, like almost everyone else in that room, to recognise what was happening. It was a slow process that he engendered. It took him a little while to fill the room up, and a while longer to erase each person within it. But it happened in the end, and there were vacant areas into which he moved. Then he began on the walls of the room, and on the house itself, phrase by phrase reducing it, abolishing it so that he grew outside us, beyond us, and passed out to the confines of the valley, and from thence up to the high bogs and the great spaces between the growing turf and the high sky. He took time away with him, and identity, and all delimiting design, and spread it out, formless and irrelevant, upon the keyboard whence a different form appeared and a new structure which had no cognisance of shape outside its own but which, because it was in part both a cure and a distillation of some constitutent faculty inadequately represented in all of us, was not destructive or arbitrary in action, but merely exclusively self-conscious and consistent.

He sat back, his hands dropping to his knees. A half-creature; the dross that remained from the thing that had created a perfect O and filled it.

◙

The structure shivered in the silence, waved and dissolved before his eyes, the content spun a little, dispersed, spent outside its cause. In the *eremikos* of his own making he stared at the black and white materials of which it was expected of him that he should construct a sufficient *oikoumenikos*, shrugged his shoulders and shut the lid of the upright bar piano.

Aaah, we murmured, aah, returning.

◙

Of necessity it was Harriet who put the first hand on the light creance that attached him to us. She moved across the room, purposefully cruel. She was the only one among us who had a child, and she acted with biological simplicity. Because of that dependent, inefficient creature she had produced, she could not afford that light line to be broken yet; she could not let him off his humanity. He was unaware of her coming, jerking upright when her hands came on his shoulders, shocked by the sudden pull of forgotten harness. 'O, Mother of God, Mother of God.'

Her hands slid down his shirt, down to his breast.

'Mother of God, Harriet, go away.'

'No.'

'That's a great gift you have, Dominic,' Willy said.

'Gift, Willy? He calls it a gift—'

We were crowding him now, closing in, curious to see what really happens at the kill. Nostrils flickered in the new smell, the smell of blood and death and lust for death. We jostled each other, shoulder to shoulder.

'Thank you, Dominic—'

'Laurie, for God's sake don't just stand there—'

'What was the second thing, Dominic, was it Scriabin—'

'Come and have a drink—'

'Did you ever hear the old girl make a noise like that?'

But Dominic was standing in the middle of the room, his lips on Harriet's mouth, and his hand tangled in her hair. His eyes were shut and shapeless, silvery tears were pouring out from under the lashes.

Naïvely, because he was a man and was crying, I thought we'd got him, between us all. But he cheated us, drawing away from Harriet, using her hair to wipe his eyes, and came to the bar.

Aah, we said, cheated at the last moment, infinitely extended upon the limit of frustration, drawing back again, covert, something ashamed—

'A round for the house, Micky,' he said, throwing his wallet across the counter, and wiping his nose on his wrist.

And everyone of us accepted it. WE ACCEPTED IT.

He turned the wireless on himself; he muttered some restrictive remark to Bill about emotional pyrotechnics, for Bill was staring at him, with his mouth open, and saying nothing. It was not until he had drunk himself, passed his fingers lightly across his lips, and pushed the long, soft hair from his wet forehead, that he turned to Willy. For God knows what reason Stephanie moved suddenly, coming between him and Willy, standing just beyond his reach, right in front of him. 'Dance with me,' she said.

Beside me I felt Matthew move restlessly. His face was anxious. 'What?' I whispered to him. I could not place him, could not see him on one side or the other.

'Can't you see? She's so brave—'

Dominic looked at my sister, in front of him. He took a step forwards and stretched out both his hands. He took her nipples, under the thin blue dress, so sharp and obvious, between his fingers and thumbs, and squeezed them slightly. Her lips parted. Behind him Micky said, 'Easy go, now, Dominic.'

The knuckles of his thumbs and fore-fingers turned white. He was pulling slightly on the tips of her nipples so that suddenly she moved forward a step, her head snapped back and her knees slowly parted and bent. He said, 'I am going to dance with Doreen,' and let go of her, walking around her, not touching her, and my sister stood in the middle of the floor with seventeen pairs of male eyes upon her ridiculously bent legs and the two little drops on the floor beneath her. I vomited all over the formica. It was the same colour as the formica. It was easy to mop up off the formica, but not off my dress or out of my mind. It was Peter who took my sister in his arms and began to dance with her, accurately, carefully, in his own fashion, as he had done at balls and parties and nightclubs for the last two years and now in the public bar of the pub.

Micky called out, 'Last round, now, drink up, last round.' The radio played *The Street where You Live* again, and

Poor little Robin and told us about the vital part the Republic was playing at the United Nations, before settling down to *Way up over the Rainbow* which everyone sang and stamped to, and the cook from the hotel cried copiously all over the Forestry Department, for she had indubitably been very frightened.

I said I was sorry to Anna for being sick beside her. Clumsily I held out my arms to her and she rose and followed me on the floor. She was very light and easy to lead, and I enjoyed it in a curious, vivid way, my shaking hands making little creases on her brilliant dress as we moved between the shoulders and the elbows, for we were both small and greatly at ease, and I was glad that the first time was not with Laurence but emotionally distinct and before the things that would happen between her and me. She must have felt something of the same sort, for she looked up at me and said, 'I was needing a rest,' and I wanted to cry for the preciousness of that remark. Our rest was short. He hadn't finished with us yet. I think it was partly reciprocal, self-perpetuating. If we had let him off after the piano, he might have let us off this. But we had goaded him into a mould which was not his shape, and because neither he nor the circumstances he had been imprisoned in were flexible, he had no choice but to smash the mould, and it was our mistake to have thought that he was not strong enough now at the end of his life to do this. More immediately, it was Willy's mistake; but Willy was acting only in concert with us and with time, and in some degree with history, and was not individually responsible. Also, how could he be expected to know the limits to which Dominic could go? Dominic, a different order of creature, at the end of its life, twisted out of shape?

Willy was standing between Dominic and Doreen. Doreen was still holding her port glass demurely in her hand, captured in her chair by the backs of Willy's legs and quite unable to get up and escape. She was leaning round Willy's buttocks to see Dominic's face. Willy was refusing to allow her to dance with him.

Suddenly Dominic changed his tactics. Anna and I weaved slowly nearer.

'Doreen,' he was saying softly, 'Is your name Maguire?'

'It is, Dominic, as you well know.'

'And was your mother's name Tessie?'

In my arms Anna shuddered and said, 'No, no, not that; Helen, dance away, dance away.' But I held her little bones against me and would only draw closer. She moaned, but I weighed ten and three-quarter stone, and I needed her frankly on my side.

'Then come and dance with me, Doreen.'

I squeezed Anna to my breasts; I remember my thumb passing rhythmically over the back of her hand, to and fro, to and fro, as the tension heightened. Her skin was cool, like satin, to and fro and to and fro.

'Would you like to dance with me, Doreen?'

I looked at Anna, and her face was yellowing, bruised and blue about the eyes and mouth. Matthew was a long way off. I turned Anna's back to him, so that he should not see her face. I thought I could keep her on her feet long enough—it was necessary now, to know.

'Willy, stand aside and let her come.'

'No, I will not let her dance with you, Dominic.'

'Willy,—'

'She's my sister, Dominic.' As he said this Willy flung his head forward, thrusting his narrow face at Dominic so that the pale eyes and the eyes that were hidden were only inches apart, and their breaths mixed, each one inhaling a fraction of the other's exhalation as their lungs refilled.

The suddenness of Willy's movement attracted attention in the closer couples. I held Anna's increasing weight tight against me as they paused to look.

Dominic held out his hand. Behind Willy Doreen took it, scrambled grotesquely around Willy's bottom and stood drawn to Dominic, gazing patiently from one to to the other. Dominic put the thumb of his right hand against her brow, the wrist against her lips, the elbow tucked into the cleft between her breasts, so that he seemed to divide her into two halves. Her eyes squinted around his hand.

'Which half, Willy? Which half is your sister and which half is mine?'

Appalled, Willy stepped back, his eyes darting from Doreen's divided face to Dominic's smile.

'Well?' Dominic took his hand from Doreen's face and carefully pulled a skein from the crown of his head, and then pulled a little from Doreen's.

'Ow!' she squealed, but he still had her by the hand. He held out the hairs to Willy. They were identical. He rubbed his fingers together and they drifted to the floor.

'This half,' he said, caressing her head like a pony's, where he had pulled the hairs out, 'this half, that shares a father with me, shall dance with me.'

As Dominic and Doreen danced away together, and Willy walked slowly to the door, Anna fainted with a thump on to the lino tiles.

▣

'Because you are an incontinent, irresponsible fool!'

'Say that again, Peter.'

'You are an incontinent, irresponsible fool, Dominic.'

Dominic did the only thing left to be done that night. With exquisite formality he turned aside to Stephanie, fumbled behind her neck and unclasped the bright gilt necklace from her throat. He weighed it for a moment or two in his hands and then tossed it down in front of Peter. It lay on the macadam of the car park, a frivolous, bright little thing. The indicator light of one of the cars was winking, and the necklace shone and dulled between their feet.

Bill said, 'Don't be a fool, Dominic.' and Stephanie, 'For God's sake stop playing the Three Musketeers. It doesn't matter any more—' and turned away from them, furious and clumsy, and Matthew, 'I forbid this' as he stooped to pick up the necklace. Dominic waited until his hand was over the silly, glittering thing and with a sort of sigh put his foot down heavily on Matthew's hand. Then he moved his weight. Matthew looked up at him, his fingers trapped under the heel of Dominic's shoe, pulled over, unable to rise, unbalanced, his huge frame grotesque in the winking light of the indicator.

From inside the car, Anna's white face peered out behind the glass, and Harriet began to open the door.

'Dominic—'

'Matthew. Matthew.' Slowly Dominic took his foot off Matthew's fingers. There was a line of blood across them. Matthew stood up, his hands empty, his face empty. He opened the door of his car and sat behind the wheel, his bloodied hand on Anna's thigh.

From the back seat Bill shouted, 'What the hell, come on.'

In the dark air Dominic's face was pale and very still

as he watched Peter stoop and pick the trinket from the car park ground. The flashing light gleamed on Stephanie's saliva still wet on his mouth.

Peter put the foolish thing in his pocket. The night was redolent with meadow-sweet and elderberry. My blood was crashing in Atlantic hammers in all my limbs, the exaltation of the Saints, the dissolution of capacity expressed in the low call of a hunting owl up on the valley sides where the air was lighter, emptier than here, and even darker. I was standing very close to Dominic, close enough to hear the tiny sounds of his body; the breath in his nostrils; the rustle of his shirt in his waistband. I could smell him. The owl hooted softly.

Peter turned and made quickly for his car. It had happened before I was aware of any intention on either of their parts. Peter drove out of the car park, swung right up the hill with Dominic in the big tourer not more than six feet behind him. Suddenly the air was full of noise; of people slamming doors and shouting; of lights and pulling hands, and I found myself dragged into the remaining car, crushed against the door which Bill locked and then slammed on me, driving the window winder deep into my side. Anna was half under me, Bill only opening the front passenger door as Matthew let out the clutch and started to move out of the car park. In the lights from the dashboard the two men's heads swayed and bobbed, Bill dragging the door shut as we swept out into the village and roared at the hill. The tail-lights of Dominic's car flashed and vanished, and Matthew's lights cut great tracks of white down the hedge and the underside of the lowering trees. 'For God's sake,' Stephanie cried. 'They won't kill each other, let them go.'

Bill and Matthew looked at each other for a second. Matthew shrugged, and suddenly I was really afraid. Anna laid her head on my breast and I moved to accommodate her, drawing her thighs up over my knees as we swayed and lurched, too closely crushed together to hurt ourselves. Beyond Stephanie, Harriet sat forwards, her arms dangling over Bill's shoulders. He reached up and held them, drawing her head to rest against his. They remained like that the whole way. There was not much talking. Peter went fast out of the valley, and I thought he was heading for the miles of bog beyond Calary, but at the last moment we saw his lights swerve right, up towards the mountains, and Dominic's immediately behind. I desperately wanted to smoke. It was very hot and very close in the back of the car, four women pressed against each other's arms and hips on the sweaty plastic seat covers. The speed became frightening; the unladen cars in front drawing further away from us; the sides of the road turning from green to the muted tones of the heather and the sharp juncus, swaying in the night air. Silhouettes of mountainous shapes heaved and reared in the sky; there were no other roads; no other cars; a stray sheep, a Holy Statue by the verge. The headlights wasted out at either side into an expanse of desolate water and thick heather, uphill and downhill and no known end to it anywhere.

Suddenly Bill said, 'He's cut his lights.'

'Who?' I asked, ignorantly. 'Why? Mightn't he have crashed—O GOD—'

'No. I saw him do it. Dominic. He'll tease Peter now, driving in his light, and Peter won't be able to see exactly where he is, because his own lights are so bright. It's an old trick but a bit dangerous up here.'

Mesmerised I watched the single lights slowing down slightly and unaccountably beginning to weave from side to side on the road.

'That's Dominic coming up on either side of him and nudging him around the road. He won't pass him or stop him; he'll just drive him wild, so that he will stop of his own accord.'

'How do you know?' Stephanie demanded, crossly.

'I've seen him do this before.'

'How did it end that time?'

Bill looked over his shoulder at her. 'You've seen him undressed. There is a knife scar in his left—'

'Shut up,' Matthew said somberly. 'No one has any knives this time. Anyway I don't believe a word of it. He's a bloody good actor, but he doesn't carry props about with him. It's all a matter of sheer bad temper, sexual jealousy and alcohol. I just want to be around in case either of the cars gets damaged. Lunatic, prep-school carry-on.' He put his foot down harder and grumbled softly to himself.

Bill leaned further forward and peered, 'Wherever are we?' he asked at last.

'Heading for Loch Bray,' Anna answered softly from my shoulder.

Loch Bray!

On either side of the car the great boulders crouched in the sweeping white light. Up on the right the mountain shoulder was close, leaning in and down on the thin road, and away to the left the boulders streamed down the heather, random, raging, insensate chaos crashing to the valley floor in a jumble of wasted strength and spent violence. Millennia ago they had ceased to move, and the heather and the heath and here and there a bent mountain ash grew up about them and secured them in perpetual imbalance. We were roaring through this petrified river of rock when suddenly Harriet cried out. Up on the shoulder of the hill, above where the road turned at right angles to the part we were on, the swaying lights of the front car suddenly doubled. There was a second in which the two sets of lights were parallel, streaming out on the rock face by the road, and then both went out. We could hear the sound in the closed car, above the engine.

'Matthew—' Harriet murmured. 'Matthew—'

No one said anything. Bill made a slight snoring sound as he breathed.

We toiled up the hill; one hundred and eighty seconds behind them.

All that had happened, in fact, was that Dominic, knowing the road from a previous visit, had remembered the lay-by which the Tourist Board had had cut into the rock, so that those who wished to enjoy the view of the little lake might do so in safety. He had come up outside Peter and simply pushed him into it. Both cars had hit the rock on the return of the lay-by hard enough to put their lights out and dent their radiators, and Dominic had punctured one front tyre. The air was still hissing out of it as we crowded round the cars. Of the two men there was no sign. We stood around the cars in the brilliant light of Matthew's lamps, unable to see into the dark outside the beams. There was no sound; no movement. Matthew went back and put off the lights. For a few seconds it was totally dark, totally quiet. Gradually I became conscious of the stars and of the stirring of the breeze in the heather. A pebble rattled, and we spun around to see the lumbering silhouette of a sheep gazing down at us from the top of the cliff. Her wool was damp with dew and smelt across the space. She turned and went quietly away. We faced out into the road again. On the other side of the road there were a few hundred yards of bog and a slight rise beyond which lay the lake. It lay in the deepest part of the larger cove in the mountain shoulder through which the road ran on the extreme edge on one side and the lake on the other. Behind the water the rock rose almost sheer, curved about it, so that the sun never so much as strokes the outermost fringes. It is perpetually dark and dreadfully cold. It was from the edge of the lake that the boulders we had crossed lower down had poured so long ago, thrust out by some wayward agency of a friendless aeon, to spill down the open side of the semi-circular recess to the green sheltered valley in the dark below us. It was too small to be majestic; even in the starlight it was merely drear.

Miserably we set off across the road to the strip of heather on the other side. No one very much wanted to find them; they would not kill each other. We heard them before we saw them, grunting, and Dominic swearing in that regular obscene way he did when he was upset. Bill and Matthew separated them, and when Dominic struggled in Matthew's giant hug he simply let him go for a second and aimed carefully, and the blow lifted Dominic right off his feet and landed him on his back in the soft heather, quite still and silent. Matthew rubbed his knuckles.

▣

It was a warm night. Despite its brevity it had been a fierce enough fight, and both Peter and Dominic were content to lie in the heather and lick their wounds and rub their bruises. There had been a glorious moment after Dominic had come round from Matthew's blow, when Peter, watching him sit up and shake his head, had advanced over the heather with his right hand extended. Dominic had watched him approach, an hysterical disbelief spreading over his face. 'My God,' he murmured in awe, 'he's just like Biggles.'

And now it was four, or half past, and the sky was lightening for the dawn over the sea. I was lying in the heather beside him, smoking one of his cigarettes. The water lapped and sucked at the peat and the tiny sand cliffs beyond our feet, dark still in its hollow, the chill of it tangible in the warm air. The dew was heavy and cool. We were sober and, I think, unafraid. Above the tiny sound of the loch we could hear Anna and Matthew making love.

'Did you not guess?' he asked gently.

'No.'

'I have known Matthew for a long time. He is a trained nurse. He looked after me once. I found him, and he came here, to Calary, to look after Anna.'

'No wonder she didn't want to marry you. I never knew Lalique could be so expensive.'

'Love is expensive, too.'

'Yes,' I said. There was nothing else to say. The rest had been spoken of enough, now.

There was a long silence. The heather-bees had not risen yet, and the quiet was eerie without them. The light shivered along the ridge of rock above the lake. I shut my eyes. Once he said 'Helen—' uncertainly, but he did not go on. After a while I moved closer to him and put my hand out. He was lying on his back with his arms over his eyes and his knees bent. I moved up between them and put my hand over the bump in his groin. He did not move. The light streak lengthened out along the rock. In the valley a wood pigeon called softly. It was warm and unexpectedly firm under my hand. I moved higher up between his thighs and laid my head on him. I ran my fingers over the seams and zip of his trousers, over his narrow hips, over the angular protuberances of the things in his pockets. My shoulders were pressed against his buttocks, and even there I could feel bone. It was warm in the heather. Slowly I turned my face into him, stroking him with my lips and my nose and my cheeks, and still he did not move. I unzipped his trousers in the end, and put my teeth into his flesh, and held the underside of his hard penis in my mouth. It was as close as I could get to her and to the thing which he had done to her, and I spoke her name about the silky loose skin, and that made him cry. When Stephanie called 'Coo-ee' from the lay-by and I heard Matthew and Anna move through the cotton grass and the squelching pools towards the road, I got up from between his legs and ran over the rise to the cars, leaving him in the heather with his throbbing organ sticking up out of his pants into the air and tears coursing down his cheeks.

◧

By the time we had turned Peter's car and Matthew's and had persuaded Peter's to start, it was fully daylight. The sheep came down to the top of the lay-by to peep shyly at our bustling, blinking their pale morning eyes and closing the long slit pupils against the rising sun. I thought we were infinitely guilty that we had bred such layers of greasy wool and fat and mutton about those delicate persons, with their tiny frail legs and pointed hooves, and was saddened to be part of such a monstrous sin. As we turned to leave I walked over to the side of the road and looked at the figure on the side of the lake. He was standing with his feet in the water and he had Harriet's penny whistle to his lips. The notes echoed off the rocks and confused the melody, making it as if several pipes were calling in fugue or counterpoint across the dark water. We left him by the water, playing *The Dance of the Courtiers* on a penny whistle.

◨

It was after six when I turned the handle of her door. There would be half an hour before the servants came upstairs. She was awake, waiting for me? There was only a loose counterpane over the sheet on top of us; thin, flimsy, white stuff, with a motif of humming birds and leaves in thread upon it. She told me it was Creole work. She said in the winter she had a Dutch blanket with hot orange and red triangles, and a pink scarf to keep the draught from her neck. She smelled of jasmine and spring flowers. We kissed, and after a little while we made love. It was very delicate, almost prudish, in full view of each other's eyes, under the white Creole cover; not at all like later times, and quite separate and distinct in my mind. When we heard the door under the stairs creak she made me go at once, and I fled up the stairs ahead of Nuala, who was alone that morning and whose legs were still swelled up.

◨

Mother put down her coffee cup with a rattle on the stone balustrade. 'Stephanie?—Helen?'

The suitcases were lined up by the open door. Grogan stood by them, waiting to put them in the cars. Topsy's father stubbed out his cigarette in an urn of lobelia. Anna watched him carefully and extracted it as soon as his back was turned. Matthew grinned at me.

'Topsy—? Mustn't keep Mother waiting; goodbye, young man, glad you've all enjoyed yourselves . . . Lady Calary—'

Topsy walked very primly to the top of the steps. She looked at Francis. 'Bye, then,' she said, airily. 'See you in London.' From inside the car she turned once to wave at him. He raised one hand, the other deep in his pocket, twitching. 'Bye,' he said softly, and suddenly smiled, very tenderly, very ruefully. He would not see her in London.

'I'm sorry the boy's not here, Monica,' Maria said. 'I understand he's punctured his car or something. To tell the truth, I don't know where he is.'

'I'm here,' he said, coming around the corner of the terrace, 'waiting for someone to give me a decent cue.' Then he stopped, staring at Mother. 'You!' he said.

'You've met, Monica.'

'Yes, Maria, we've met.' She turned her head; she had a way of turning her head, very slowly, so that no other part of her moved, just the long slender neck. Quite often she blinked very slowly as she did this. She did it this time. She was dressed entirely in blue and green. She was outrageous. She said, 'Don't come any closer, Laurie darling. You are quite filthy and I have no doubt that you smell of marsh gas.'

He could blink slowly, too, a caress of the lashes. He made no other reply, but his lips moved together.

He was barefooted, with his trousers rolled half way up the calves. He had no shirt on, and a tin whistle stuck out of his pocket.

'Tuesday, then, in the Museum bookshop,' I whispered.

'I'll be there, don't worry.'

'Promise, Laurence, promise you'll be there.'

'I promise I'll be there.'

'You won't forget, or be run over, or—'

'I won't forget, and I will issue all the old sheep with klaxons so that I will hear them coming—'

'You are teasing me—promise again—'

'Helen, are you ready?'

'Yes, yes, I'm coming. Promise,' I hissed.

'I promise.'

I could not kiss her. I shook hands formally, until Tuesday. Her fingers had round tips; I was not able to raise them to my lips here, now, as Dominic did my mother's.

As we went down the steps to the car Maria called, 'Monica, if you hear of a liver-in, let me know. My housemaid is leaving.'

Mother grimaced sympathetically. 'Not likely,' she muttered. 'What do you think I'm looking for all these years? I will,' she called.

'Doreen?' I asked, turning on the bottom step.

'Who else. Going to England, of all places to join the bloody W.R.N.S. Mother of God!' She made a clumsy, half-military gesture.

'Come again, Helen, it's been good—' Anna smiled.

I would come again.

Stephanie got into the front of the car with Mother. I scrambled into the back while Grogan watched my thighs through the window as he held the driver's door for my mother.

I could see her almost all the way down the rhododen-drons, against the window. I thought I could see her for much longer than that.

It was very quiet in the car. When we were through Enniskerry and climbing out the far side of the valley, Mother said, 'I'm sorry about that, girls.'

Stephanie said, 'It flatters me,' and grinned into the driving mirror.

'It does?'

'Very much.'

Mother began to laugh and Stephanie with her. It was a gentle, burbling sound of two women in private. I had never heard Mother and Stephanie laugh together like that before. When we were through the Scalp Mother wiped her eyes on a little hankie and said, 'Well, I don't know what you'll think, but I am going to marry again.' She giggled and went on, 'I think November—the chrysanthemums, you know.'

Stephanie clutched her tummy, 'O, Mother, you are! Can we have a double wedding? I'm going to be married in November, too.'

Mother put her head on one side. 'Do you think it would be quite decorous?' and then, 'STEPHANIE! Who to?'

'Peter, of course.'

'Oh. Of course. Yes, so obvious. Dear goodness, O, Stephanie I am GLAD—' and they laughed and laughed until Mother stopped the car in the middle of the road and hugged her, and they hugged and pealed with laughter at the prospect of being married women.

'We must have a serious talk,' Mother said, waving a milk lorry, two cars and a tractor head-on into a bus and a Sunbeam Alpine. No one was hurt. 'A very serious talk.'

'I think you are in a vulnerable place,' I said hesitantly,

'not to say inconvenient for other people.'

'You are quite right, dear. I shall move on.'

The mood of hilarity was destroyed. They looked uncomfortably at each other. They had forgotten about me. They had been so pretty laughing together that I said, 'I won't be going back to school, now. So I can come to the wedding.'

'What do you mean?' they asked in unison.

'I am going to be a librarian. I am not going to go to Oxford. I am going to take a small flat in town and do a short course in Dublin, and then I shall go to London next year.'

By that time Anna and Matthew would be married and Laurence free. It did not seem too long a time if I could stay in Dublin. In a flat of my own.

'Could you manage the rent for me, Mother?'

'Mother, who are YOU going to marry?' Stephanie said suddenly, scowling.

'Marc-Raoul, of course.'

'Oh. Of course. Yes,' and we all three laughed.

'When will you be going to France?'

'Well, if Helen has a flat and you are married, I see no reason why I shouldn't go straight after the wedding. I've done lesson twenty-five already,' she added obscurely.

'Paris?' I asked, seeing the Flea Market and the Cluny and the wine spilled on the wide zinc counters.

'No, no, not Paris. South. The Garonne.'

Somewhere to dry out if the houseboat sank next summer. I began to laugh, too. We were hysterical as we passed the bus stop. Willy Maguire was standing by it. He had a brown suit on, and shiny shoes, and a big, roped suitcase was on the ground beside him. His face was empty of any hate or vengeance. He looked like a deprived ox.

DOMINIC

SO YOU ARE GOING, are you. Walking out. Leaving me after three years. Don't give me all that crap about there not being anyone else. You're not that sensitive, lovely, and I should know. Whoever they are, I hope you have a lovely time with her/him.

That was a lie, you know. I'm not morbid. I've just been in love. And you couldn't understand that and couldn't bear it. You rant about self-pity and self-justification; Christ, I only gave you a story to read—what's so psychological about that? You're always asking questions, those were the answers.

When I am alone I will think about the way you walked out, and how you couldn't take it that I had loved Lyn like that and had four years in Bordeaux with Laurence. I miss her—I might even go down there and try and patch things up with her. Funny how things repeat themselves. She had the same hard streak when it came to the way I felt that summer. You can't understand what it was like feeling the pull of him, against nature; and then finding out that it was he who had taken Lyn away, destroyed her forever, banging her up there on the downs, like he did anyone who could take their knickers off quick enough; my sister, the whore at the theatre, my mother—my Lady—

Can't you see? She was so clean, always; even her Everyday Dresses were clean—

Sometimes, on the bad nights I wonder if he left her in some low pub in Pewsey or Devizes with her knees splayed and her tits like stalks—

It takes a long time to organise hatred, Aileen.

Remember to leave your front door key behind.

Helen

Laurence Dominic Marie SanFé Laurence Dominic
Marie SanFé Laurence Dominic Marie SanFé Laurence
Dominic Marie SanFé Laurence Dominic
Dominic
O Dominic Dominic DOMINIC

O GOD